Death at the Sanatorium

Ragnar Jónasson is an international number one bestselling author who has sold over three million books in thirty-four countries worldwide. He was born in Reykjavík, Iceland, where he also works as an investment banker and teaches copyright law at Reykjavík University.

He has previously worked on radio and television, including as a TV news reporter for the Icelandic National Broadcasting Service, and, from the age of seventeen, has translated fourteen of Agatha Christie's novels. His critically acclaimed international bestseller *The Darkness* is soon to be a major TV series, and Ridley Scott will be producing *Outside* as a feature film.

By the same author

The Darkness

The Island

The Mist

The Girl Who Died

Outside

Reykjavík (*with Katrín Jakobsdóttir*)

Death at the Sanatorium

RAGNAR JÓNASSON

Translated from the Icelandic
by Victoria Cribb

PENGUIN MICHAEL JOSEPH

UK | USA | Canada | Ireland | Australia
India | New Zealand | South Africa

Penguin Michael Joseph is part of the Penguin Random House group of companies whose addresses can be found at global.penguinrandomhouse.com

First published in Iceland with the title *Hvítidauði* by Veröld Publishing 2019
First published in Great Britain 2024
002

Set in 13.75/16.25pt Garamond MT Std
Typeset by Jouve (UK), Milton Keynes
Printed and bound in Great Britain by Clays Ltd, Elcograf S.p.A.

The authorized representative in the EEA is Penguin Random House Ireland, Morrison Chambers, 32 Nassau Street, Dublin D02 YH68

A CIP catalogue record for this book is available from the British Library

HARDBACK ISBN: 978–0–241–49363–2
TRADE PAPERBACK ISBN: 978–0–241–49364–9

www.greenpenguin.co.uk

To Dr Helgi Johannsson – who lent Helgi his name

Helgi's Golden Age Reading List

The Murder of Roger Ackroyd by Agatha Christie, 1926
The Dutch Shoe Mystery by Ellery Queen, 1931
Peril at End House by Agatha Christie, 1932
Enter a Murderer by Ngaio Marsh, 1935
A Puzzle for Fools by Patrick Quentin, 1940

'Behind my shoulder death awaits.'

– Jóhann Sigurjónsson (1880–1919),
from the poem 'The Cup'

2012

Helgi

The despairing silence was broken.

There was someone at the front door, knocking loudly.

Helgi got to his feet.

He had been sitting on the sofa with a detective novel, trying to calm himself down before bed by losing himself in a fictional world, but now the peace was over.

He and Bergthóra rented a basement flat in an old house not far from Reykjavík's Laugardalur area. The whole house was rented out, the flat upstairs occupied by a couple with two children. Apparently the landlord lived overseas.

Helgi didn't get on particularly well with the other tenants, who had a tendency to be rude and interfering, as if their rights took precedence just because they lived in the larger half of the house. As a result, relations between the basement and upstairs were strictly limited and frosty at best.

Helgi was afraid it was the neighbour at the door now,

sticking his nose in yet again. But there was another, worse possibility.

He moved reluctantly towards the hall. The sitting room was cosy, the walls lined from floor to ceiling with books – his books; a comfy armchair by the shelves and a decent-sized sofa in front of the television. There were scented candles on the coffee table, but Helgi hadn't lit them. Not this time. He'd put a record on the stereo, though; a real vinyl one. The stereo was new and connected up to the home cinema, but the records he played were old jazz LPs that had belonged to his father. The heavy banging on the front door broke through the soothing music, wrecking the tranquil atmosphere that had settled over the flat.

Hell, Helgi thought.

He had reached the hall when there was another round of hammering, even louder this time. He drew a sharp breath, then took hold of the handle, pausing briefly to collect himself before he turned the latch and opened the door.

Outside stood a uniformed police officer, a broad-shouldered young man in his mid-twenties, with strong features. He was standing in the glow of the outside light, brightly illuminated in the evening darkness, wearing a look of grim determination, as if he were anticipating a fight. Helgi didn't recognize him. In the shadows, a little behind him, stood another officer. He seemed more at his ease, judging by his stance, though Helgi couldn't make out his face.

'Good evening,' said the illuminated officer. His voice

wasn't as authoritative as Helgi had been expecting; in fact he thought he detected a faint tremor. Perhaps the determined set of the man's features was just a ploy to disguise his nerves. Perhaps it was his first shift. 'Helgi? Helgi Reykdal?'

Although Helgi, now in his early thirties, wasn't that much older than the man asking his name, he sensed he had the advantage over this young officer.

'Helgi Reykdal, yes, that's right. Why, what's up?' he asked smoothly, shifting the balance of power slightly.

'We've received – that's to say . . .' The young policeman hesitated, as Helgi had guessed he might. 'A complaint has been received . . .'

Helgi interrupted. 'A complaint? Who from?' He wasn't going to let himself appear flustered.

'Well, we . . . er, we can't reveal that.'

'There's a bloke upstairs,' Helgi said, smiling. 'He's a bloody nuisance, always complaining. I reckon he must be unhappily married or something. You can't so much as raise your voice, or, I don't know, you can't even turn up the TV, without him banging on the floor with a broom handle. And now I see he's called the police.'

'He heard a loud altercation . . .' The young officer broke off mid-sentence, clearly realizing that he had said too much. 'That's to say, we received a complaint . . .'

'You already mentioned that,' Helgi said, unfazed.

'A complaint about a loud disturbance at this address – a quarrel and screaming. More serious than your average row.'

At that moment the other police officer emerged from

the shadows, looked Helgi straight in the eye, then took a step closer. 'You know, I thought the name sounded familiar,' he said to Helgi.

The moment he got a good look at the man, Helgi recognized him. They had sometimes worked the same shifts in the Reykjavík police last year, though they didn't actually know each other that well.

'The name's Reimar,' the officer said. 'Were you just temping with us over the summer or were you with us for longer?'

'That's right, I temped for a bit after finishing my police training,' Helgi replied. 'Then I went on to do a post-grad degree in criminology.'

'Oh, yes, that was it,' Reimar said. 'I seem to remember someone telling me. In the UK, wasn't it? I've often thought about it myself, you know – continuing my education.'

Helgi nodded. He was still standing at his ease in the doorway, as if he were the one in charge. 'Strictly speaking, I'm still a student. I just need to finish my dissertation, but it made more sense for us to move back to Iceland. My partner got offered a good job, you see.' Helgi smiled.

'Nice to run into you again,' Reimar said. 'Well, not in the most desirable circumstances, obviously. So you're having problems with your neighbour, are you?'

'Yes, you can say that again. The man's a bloody idiot. It's only a rented flat, though, so we'll be moving sooner or later.'

'He heard a disturbance,' the younger officer said slowly.

'That's right, my partner and I had a bit of a disagreement, but nothing to call the police about. Like I said, you recently in connection with his dissertation. Deaths at a sanatorium . . .

He read a few more pages but couldn't focus. Perhaps the book just wasn't very good, but he thought it more likely that the police, or rather his upstairs neighbour, had unsettled him. Maybe it would be better to put the book aside for now, to finish at the weekend, and try to get some sleep instead. He would bed down on the sofa, as usual after one of their rows. It was always him who had to make the sacrifice.

He laid the book gently on the coffee table; he always took great care of the collection. They were his treasures, these old detective novels, even though they might not fetch much of a price if sold.

Helgi was eager to get to sleep; as a rule, he had no problems dropping off and he really needed to gather his strength for the job of finishing his dissertation. The subject was so unusual that he had been rather surprised when his tutor in the UK had agreed to it.

A blanket and a cushion would have to take the place of a pillow and duvet tonight, but that didn't matter; he was used to it and the flat was perfectly warm.

Helgi took off his white shirt and hung it over the back of a chair.

His heart missed a beat.

Just as well his colleagues in the police hadn't noticed the small red bloodstain on the sleeve.

1983

Tinna

Tinna ploughed through the rain, head down, clutching her coat tightly around herself. The sky was unusually grey and in the downpour everything seemed to merge into one: clouds, pavement; even the houses appeared drab and colourless. All other sounds had faded into the background and the only thing she could hear was the drumming of the rain, but then there was hardly another soul about in the streets of Akureyri at a quarter to seven on a Saturday morning. It was a relief to reach the car and get inside out of the wet.

Tinna was young; it wasn't that long since she had graduated from her nursing degree. As a native of the north Icelandic town of Akureyri, she had initially been over the moon to get a job there after finishing her studies in Reykjavík, since it meant she could be close to her parents and extended family. In practice, though, it had been a bit of a comedown to return to the quiet little town on the fjord after a taste of life in the big city. Although it was known as the capital of the north, Akureyri had a population of only thirteen thousand people, and Tinna was already finding it claustrophobic to be surrounded again by the faces she had grown up with. If she wanted to expand her social circle, she was beginning to realize that she would have to head back south at some point.

But, for now, the job at the old sanatorium wasn't bad, though the place was eight kilometres out of town, so not exactly within walking distance of her flat. Her work wasn't quite as demanding as she could have wished either, but she supposed it represented a decent enough start to her career. Although the tuberculosis patients were long gone – the last one had departed before Tinna was born – the hospital was still overshadowed by its association with the disease they used to call the 'white death'. And the locals still spoke of the place with an awed dread, despite the hospital standing empty, with the sole exception of the wing where Tinna worked. The department had no patients but was concerned with diagnostics, research and the development of workflow processes in health care. Meanwhile, a bunch of people down south in Reykjavík were busy debating the best possible use the old sanatorium buildings could be put to in the future.

Tinna had gone to bed late, having sat up half the night with her old friend Bigga, and now she was fighting off tiredness. The weather didn't help. How she would have loved to turn round and go home, crawl under her duvet and fall asleep again with the ticking of the rain in her ears. Perhaps she should have called in sick, but that wouldn't have created a very good impression. She would just have to grit her teeth and slog through this morning's shift, then have a coffee and hope the day would gradually pick up after that.

It was her job to arrive first, switch on the lights, make the coffee, and get everything up and running for the day. She was supposed to be there on the dot of seven, an hour before the other two nurses, Yrsa and Elísabet, came in. They were both more experienced than her, in fact the older woman, Yrsa, had several decades of experience under her belt and couldn't have much time left before she retired. Like Tinna, she had begun her career at the sanatorium, but, unlike Tinna, she was clearly intending to finish it there too. Of course, Yrsa would have had to deal with far more challenging duties when she was young, as the hospital had still been full of TB patients back then. Tinna liked to think of herself as a level-headed person, but even she sometimes had the fancy that the ghosts of the departed still roamed the empty corridors. She had never actually been aware of anything herself, but, all the same, she often felt uneasy in the building, especially when she was alone.

The surrounding mountains were shrouded in cloud today, the waters of Eyjafjördur grey, as she drove out of town through the teeming rain, her wipers swishing, past the little airport and on up the valley until eventually she reached the hospital turn-off. The white buildings loomed up, standing in splendid isolation on their hillside above the river, overshadowed by a garden of mature pines in this otherwise bare landscape. The main block was an austere, three-storey edifice, its long rows of windows dark and empty these days. More than ever, it reminded Tinna of an old sanatorium in a horror movie.

She dashed through the rain from the car to the entrance, eager to get under cover. In her relief at being inside, it took her a moment or two to realize that the door hadn't been locked, as it usually was. Had someone forgotten to close up yesterday evening? The lights in the hall were on too. That was strange.

It was probably Yrsa's fault. Just as well, since that meant she wouldn't be able to take it out on anyone else. In spite of her quiet, unassuming demeanour, Yrsa could be surprisingly quick to fly off the handle when something happened to displease her. Tinna had recently seen her give Elísabet a vicious tongue-lashing for a minor mistake, though Elísabet had been working there far longer than Tinna. It seemed that Tinna was still in Yrsa's good books, for what it was worth, though they were very far from what you might call friends. In fact, Tinna knew next to nothing about Yrsa beyond the fact that she had worked as a nurse for many years. They never discussed anything that you might call personal. Yrsa had never asked Tinna about her family or her interests, and certainly hadn't revealed anything about her own. The older woman tended to be taciturn and unforthcoming. She went around with a dour face, as though she'd been forced to watch too much suffering over the years, which was no doubt true. Tinna pictured her: small, always dressed in a starched white uniform, her short, silver-grey hair framing a square face, her eyes distant, as though her thoughts were wandering among old memories, dwelling on all the patients who had lost the battle with the merciless disease. If there was one thing Tinna was determined to avoid, it was being stuck here for her entire working life like Yrsa. As far as she was concerned, this job was no more than a springboard; in future she wanted to specialize in more demanding work at a larger hospital.

Tinna headed up the staircase, walking slowly to begin with, conscious of every echoing footstep, uncomfortably aware that she was totally alone in this wing of the building. She was always a little spooked in the morning. She quickened her pace slightly, as she normally did when approaching the upper landing, and the echoes grew louder, more overwhelming, seeming to reverberate all around her. Tinna breathed easier once she was upstairs. Her new yellow coat was soaking wet, and she took it off carefully, anxious to avoid getting rainwater all over the floor, but a small puddle formed under the pegs anyway. Still, what did it matter when you could bet that it would be her job to wipe it up?

The door to Yrsa's office was standing ajar. That too was unusual, and again Tinna felt a prickle of discomfort. It occurred to her with a jolt that she might not be alone after all. Perhaps Yrsa had come in at the crack of dawn and that's why the front door had been unlocked and the door to her office was open.

Tinna called out, though not very loudly: 'Yrsa, are you in already?'

She didn't move but stood quite still by the row of pegs, watching the water dripping from her yellow coat on to the tiles. She expected Yrsa to answer with her usual brusqueness, then order her to bring a coffee, adding, 'And don't hang about.' But the only sound she could hear was the quiet, muffled plinking of the drops as they landed on the tiles, a sure sign that Yrsa was not on the premises.

Tinna decided to double-check anyway. She was still feeling unsettled, some primitive instinct warning her that something was wrong. She walked over to Yrsa's office and hovered for a moment or two outside her door before pushing it fully open.

Her immediate reaction was surprise, just for a split second, before this gave way to fear.

Tinna saw at once that Yrsa was dead and realized in the same instant that there had been nothing natural about her demise. In spite of this, she went over and cautiously pressed her fingers to Yrsa's neck to check for any signs of life. There was no pulse.

Tinna knew in that moment that she would never forget the expression on Yrsa's face. Tinna had seen dead bodies before during her short career, but this was different. There was nothing peaceful about Yrsa. She looked as though she had fought to the bitter end; as though she hadn't been remotely ready to relinquish this life. Yet it occurred to Tinna that Yrsa hadn't exactly had much to live for. The callous thought flashed through her head as she tried to take in what she was seeing, her mind simultaneously struggling to resist the horror.

Yrsa had often claimed, rather proudly, that the antique

wooden desk in her office was her personal property – an old family heirloom. *The desk my father always used to work at*, she'd said. And now she was lying across the desk, her grey hair like a halo around her head. The dark red pool of blood on the desktop made a macabre contrast with the dead woman's greyish skin. It took Tinna a little while to grasp what she was seeing. At first, she assumed the blood had come from Yrsa's head, from a blow perhaps, or a bullet, but then, with a sort of sick horror, she noticed that two of Yrsa's fingers had been cut off. Her maimed hand rested on the desk, the gory fingers lying nearby.

Tinna took a step backwards, then another, and averted her eyes, heaving a deep, shaky breath. She resisted a powerful impulse to run out of the room, curiosity overcoming her common sense. This was a kind of test. If she wanted to work as a nurse, she would have to get used to worse sights than this. She forced herself to look back at the dead woman.

She hadn't been mistaken.

The thumb and index finger of Yrsa's right hand had been amputated, and now there was no question that this was the source of the blood, which must mean, Tinna realized, that the mutilation had been carried out while Yrsa was still alive.

Her skin crawled at the thought.

Then it flashed into her mind that she herself might be in danger.

She threw a glance over her shoulder, feeling the adrenaline pumping through her veins. There was no one behind her, but then Yrsa's office was quite small, so no one could be hiding in there. Tinna stood still, straining her ears, but all she could hear was the habitual creaking and groaning of the old building. She was alone. The only living soul in this wing, the only living soul in the whole hospital.

She left Yrsa's office, being careful not to touch anything else, though she knew her prints would be on the handle from when she had pushed the door open. It couldn't be helped.

Her next step was to call the police. There was a phone on Yrsa's desk, but using that was out of the question. She was afraid of touching anything in the room, for fear of spoiling evidence. There was another phone in the director's office, but his door was shut and Tinna wouldn't dream of barging in there uninvited.

She hurried downstairs to reception, where there was a phone that the other members of staff were allowed to use. Resisting the urge to flee the building, she told herself that she had to call the police immediately; she had no alternative. Before picking up the receiver, she wondered if she might be destroying any fingerprints, but it seemed unlikely, and anyway the most urgent thing was to get the police over here. She was about to dial the number when she realized that she couldn't remember it. Because it wasn't every day that she had to ring the police; in fact, this was the first time she had ever done it. She glanced around, searching in vain for a telephone directory, and eventually found last year's in a drawer. Having looked up the number, she made the call. It was answered almost immediately.

'Police.' A gravelly male voice.

For a moment, fear constricting her throat, Tinna couldn't stammer out a word.

'Police,' repeated the voice.

She coughed and drew a deep breath. 'Yes . . . yes, hello, my name's Tinna and I'm calling from the old sanatorium, I . . .' She broke off, frantically trying to find the right words.

'Yes? Has something happened?'

'Yes . . . er, yes, I think a woman who works here . . . I think she's been murdered.'

1950

Ásta

Ásta had seen so much death and suffering during the twenty years she had been working at the sanatorium. Far more than anyone should have to. She'd started there in 1930, only four years after the hospital had opened. Those were the bad years, when tuberculosis had been one of the biggest killers in Iceland, just as it seemed to be on the retreat in neighbouring countries. The main treatment then had been to isolate patients from the public and provide them with plenty of rest and fresh air, but the big sanatorium outside Reykjavík could no longer house all the cases and the decision had been taken to build a new one up north, in the countryside outside Akureyri.

The disease was pitiless, selecting its victims indiscriminately but especially affecting the young. The torment some of the patients had to endure was indescribable, the only available treatments were brutal, and often there was nothing she could do but try to make their existence more bearable, in cases where the patients had nothing to look forward to but oblivion, to dying long before their time.

Yes, it had been worst in the early years, but over the course of her career the number of cases had gone down and the disease had become more treatable. These days fewer patients died, though sadly they couldn't save everyone, yet there were hopeful signs that victory was just around the corner.

The doctors, at least, gave the impression of being more optimistic than before, especially the director, Fridjón, who was part of the new generation, not yet forty. Brilliant and energetic, the son of a respected lawyer in Akureyri and brother of the local chief constable, he was a man with a contribution to make, yet instead of heading to the capital, he had chosen to employ his talents here in the north at the sanatorium, where good men could really make a difference. Ásta sensed that there were better times ahead and that a proper cure would soon be discovered for this cruel disease.

That day, a grey, wet Monday, had been particularly harrowing.

A new patient had been admitted to the ward. It was always bad news when someone was admitted to what she privately thought of as death's waiting room. To make matters worse, the boy was only five years old. Five . . . She remembered when her own son was five, a little angel, innocent but mischievous. For one brief moment, looking through the glass partition into the little boy's sickroom and meeting his tear-filled eyes, she had seen her son's eyes reflected in them. Her heart had gone out to the poor little mite and she prayed he would have the strength to fight. Because she knew that the illness needn't be a death sentence; she had seen so many examples of the opposite, seen patients rally after a gruelling battle and get a second chance at life. The disease almost invariably attacked the lungs, and those who survived never recovered their former physical strength, but at least they were alive. That was all that mattered. She had seen how the patients who got the better of TB went on to embrace life afterwards. She had seen the hope in their eyes, and perhaps that was why she hadn't thrown in the towel; why she had stuck it out in this punishing job for twenty years. Hope lent her strength and added purpose to her life.

Then there were days like this one, when despair got the better of her. Seeing a little boy faced with such overwhelming odds. It wasn't as if his life had been easy before either, from what she had heard. His mother was an unmarried alcoholic with two sons, this little boy and an older brother, no doubt by a different father.

Ásta didn't have many years left in her job. She meant to stop working as soon as she could and enjoy a contented retirement with her husband, watching her grandchildren grow up. She had done her best, she felt, to nurse the patients and help make the world a slightly better place. She had never looked for advancement, and never got it. For a while, two years back, she had thought she might be asked to take on the position of matron when it became available. But the call never came and a young woman by the name of Yrsa had been appointed instead. She got on fine with Yrsa, though they didn't mix at all outside work, but she found the age gap uncomfortably wide. Yrsa, who was hardly more than thirty, might as well have been her daughter, but now Ásta had to take her orders from her. Of course, she had learnt to live with that, like everything else, but Yrsa's appointment was probably yet another reason behind her decision to take retirement as soon as she could. Everything had its time.

Poor little boy. Her thoughts returned to the child. There were patients at the sanatorium who were far gone, who it was her duty to nurse; people she had grown attached to. The boy wasn't even her responsibility, not directly, yet she felt a strong bond with him, perhaps because he reminded her of her son, and she was determined to keep an eye on him to make sure he was all right and didn't become isolated. He was a happy, boisterous child who enjoyed making up stories. Today, for instance, his father had been a policeman or rather a chief constable. She had said, 'Oh, is he, dear?' and let him believe it. Perhaps he was expecting his father to come and save him from the disease. Tomorrow his father might be a fireman or a cowboy.

Sometimes she knew better than the younger members of staff; she knew how important the personal touch was for her patients, because the will to live could be as crucial a factor in deciding the patient's fate as the illness itself.

Yes, Ásta had performed her job conscientiously for twenty years. She'd always gone out of her way to be kind to others, and she would go on doing so until it was time for her to step aside and make way for a new generation.

2012

Helgi

It was past nine o'clock by the time Helgi woke up, and Bergthóra had already left for work. He'd slept well, not stirring all night, but then the sofa made quite a comfortable bed when required. Bergthóra hadn't woken him to say goodbye, but then that was par for the course.

What he really wanted was to read a few more chapters of his detective novel about Peter Duluth, but instead he made himself get up. There were too many distractions now that he had moved back to Iceland and didn't have a job; it would be easy to fall into the habit of staying up all night and sleeping all day, achieving nothing, but that wasn't an option. He had always been organized and diligent, but in the present circumstances he would need to exert all his self-discipline if he were to finish his dissertation as soon as possible.

A decision had to be made about his future. He was conscious that he should be overjoyed to have choices, to be a young man with his whole life ahead of him, but the uncertainty made him insecure, even a little apprehensive.

His tutor in the UK had put him in touch with a British law firm that did forensic work for clients, and they had not only shown an interest in him but actually offered him a job. He had been quite excited by the idea, as he'd always wanted to try working abroad and now that door was open. But when he wanted to accept, Bergthóra had refused to countenance it, and the resulting quarrel still hadn't been fully resolved. First, she had said that if they were going to continue living abroad, they might as well move somewhere warmer, though she didn't say where and, more importantly, he hadn't been offered work anywhere further south. Then she'd said that she didn't want to give up her job in Iceland. She had taken a career break to go to the UK with him while he was studying, but it had always been understood that the arrangement was temporary, and now that she was back in Iceland she had resumed her old managerial position. She was a social welfare officer, and, in his opinion, her job put her under a worrying amount of pressure, even compared to his experience of police work. Sometimes he wished she was in a different profession.

Then there was the other job offer. Helgi had got a phone call from the head of the police department responsible for investigating serious crimes such as manslaughter and grievous bodily harm. Helgi had no experience of CID work as his duties as a summer temp had been far more routine, involving a bit of everything. The man had rung him out of the blue, having presumably heard about him on the grapevine, since Helgi had performed extremely well in his studies abroad and also had a number of contacts in the police back in Iceland. He was forced to recognize that if his dream of working in the UK wasn't to be, then this would be the perfect consolation prize – working on complex investigations in Reykjavík CID. Following the phone call, Helgi had gone to the police station for an interview, and it was all up to him now. He could start work later this year if he liked; he just needed to come to a decision.

Of course, he and Bergthóra had talked it over, and she'd made her wishes plain, repeatedly declaring that she couldn't understand why he hadn't already accepted the job here in Reykjavík. 'They won't wait for ever, Helgi,' she kept saying. But there wasn't actually that much of a hurry. Not only was Helgi obviously the man the head of department wanted for the job, but he hadn't been put under any time pressure. All he wanted at the moment was to savour his freedom for a few more months and keep his dream of working in the UK alive a little while longer. He needed time to settle back into life in Reykjavík and accept the fact that his career would begin here and, in all likelihood, end here as well.

At the time he'd left to go abroad, the situation in Iceland had been dire in the wake of the banking crisis, but he had come home to find the country in recovery. Tourism was booming thanks to the weakened currency, which had turned Iceland from a punitively expensive destination to an attractive place to holiday. All around him he could sense the increased optimism in the air after the soul searching and pessimism of the post-crash years, when it had seemed that everyone had stopped making plans for the future.

Perhaps making a life here wouldn't be so bad after all. He wouldn't be bored working for CID; he knew he had an aptitude for his new job, and of course he always had his detective novels to retreat into when the pressures of daily life became too intense.

He had made a start on his dissertation. It had proved fairly easy to get permission to access the police files, on condition that his study wouldn't be available for public access straight away. Presumably it had helped that the case was almost thirty years old. 'The Deaths at the Sanatorium' was how some of the newspapers had referred to it at the time – it even sounded like a golden-age mystery. Naturally, Helgi had studied all the news reports and articles he could lay his hands on. Although the deaths had been shocking when they happened in 1983, they felt so remote now that reading about them was like reading an old crime novel, and the experience was similar when he leafed through the yellowing typewritten reports in the police archives. Real, flesh-and-blood people had lost their lives in tragic circumstances, but to Helgi it was above all an interesting puzzle. The case had appealed to him partly because of its link to his home town of Akureyri. The imposing buildings of the old sanatorium were a familiar sight to the locals, and he had been aware of the deaths there for a while, since long before he decided to write about them. During his post-grad studies in the UK he had got the idea of using his dissertation as a chance to delve into the historical inquiry. Viewed with a modern eye, there were some obvious question marks hanging over the conclusions of the original police investigation, and the motive remained tantalizingly obscure. Armed with the theories he'd learnt on his criminology course, he meant to conduct a thorough, academic analysis of one of the most notorious murder cases in recent Icelandic history.

But what attracted him most, of course, about 'The Deaths at the Sanatorium', was that nearly thirty years later, as far as he could see, the mystery remained unsolved.

1983

Tinna

Yrsa had been murdered.

Of course, the fact hadn't escaped Tinna when she discovered the body, as any other explanation would have been pretty much impossible. As soon as the police arrived at the scene, they had closed the department and escorted Tinna from the building. A young female officer had been detailed to look after her and comfort her, though she hadn't actually needed any comforting. The shock had been quick to pass. It wasn't as though she'd been fond of Yrsa; Tinna hadn't even liked her much, so the woman was no loss to her. Naturally, Tinna felt sorry for Yrsa, especially as it appeared that she'd been subjected to agonizing torture, but the fact was that life in the department was bound to be easier now that Yrsa was out of the picture. It was fairly clear that Elísabet would take over her role, and that was a pleasing prospect. Tinna and Elísabet got on very well together – you could almost call them friends – and Elísabet was only thirty-five, much closer in age to Tinna than Yrsa had been.

Come to think of it, Elísabet had bitched so much about Yrsa in the short time Tinna had been working there that the thought did briefly cross Tinna's mind, though not very seriously, that Elísabet might have taken matters into her own hands. 'She's stuck in the past,' Elísabet had complained more than once, or words to that effect. But it was one thing to talk like that, another to commit a violent crime . . . No, it was out of the question. Some disturbed person must have done it in a moment of madness – some outsider; that had to be the explanation.

'As you've probably guessed, Yrsa was murdered,' the policeman said. Such a nice guy. Far too young to be in charge of a major investigation like this, Tinna thought. He had come up from Reykjavík, so she'd never encountered him before. Noticing that there was no ring on his finger, she wondered if she could engineer a meeting with him in happier circumstances, once the case was closed. Was it possible that Yrsa's death might actually lead to something positive?

'Yes, well, I had my suspicions,' she answered in a low, quavering voice, trying to give the impression that she was still recovering from the sight of the body. 'It was . . . it was so awful.'

The policeman, who had introduced himself as Sverrir, nodded.

'Sverrir,' she said then, relishing the chance to say his name, 'do the police know what happened?'

The question seemed to catch him unprepared. Perhaps he had been primed to ask all the questions rather than answer any himself.

'It's being looked into. I'm afraid I can't say any more at present.'

'I saw that two of her fingers had been cut off. The thumb and the index finger, I thought. Do you have any idea why?'

'We can't really go into details at this stage, Tinna,' he said awkwardly.

If anything, she thought, Sverrir was even more attractive when he was embarrassed and unsure of himself.

'I've read the statement you made to the police when the body was found.' He paused, then asked: 'Is there anything you'd like to add to your story?'

Tinna shook her head. She reckoned she'd given an impressively lucid description of the events, considering the circumstances. 'I don't think there's much I can add.'

'You mentioned that the door downstairs was unlocked. Was that unusual?'

'Yes, very unusual. There aren't actually any patients here at the moment as we're only carrying out research and administrative work and waiting for instructions about what the future set-up is going to look like. We mainly undertake jobs for the County Hospital – really, we should be based there, but they're keen to keep some of the operations here; for political reasons, I expect. I always get in first in the mornings, so I was a bit disconcerted to find the door unlocked. It made me wary, though of course I had no idea what had happened. I couldn't have begun to imagine what I'd find – but I did feel uneasy, all the same.'

'I see,' Sverrir said, looking thoughtful. 'Could you run through the names of all the people who have keys to the building?'

'She – er – Yrsa could have let someone in herself,' Tinna pointed out.

'Of course, we're not ruling anything out. But we have to start by eliminating the people who worked with her.'

'You mean people like me?' she asked, a little archly, then realized from Sverrir's stern expression that he found her tone inappropriate.

'Exactly,' he said.

'Well, there are five of us working there at the moment, apart from Yrsa. Me, the two doctors, Elísabet, and the caretaker. None of us likely murderers, if you want my opinion.'

'Two doctors, right. Thorri's one of them, isn't he?'

'Thorri, yes – he's the younger one. He seems like a decent guy, a good doctor,' she said, though in truth she wasn't all that keen on the man. He was arrogant and difficult, and although he was still relatively young, he had old-fashioned attitudes about doctors being the be all and end all, superior to everyone else. Whereas the old doctor, the director, Fridjón, was the complete opposite. Fridjón had been a fixture at the sanatorium for decades, longer even than Yrsa, and was approaching retirement now, yet he was so kind and approachable. Always ready to help, and polite to Tinna from the first day. If someone had to die, she was glad that at least it hadn't been him.

'Did Thorri have any connection to Yrsa?' Sverrir asked.

'Connection to Yrsa? How do you mean? They were colleagues, obviously, but I don't think they knew each other outside work.' Leaning towards him, Tinna added confidingly: 'Yrsa wasn't very sociable. I can tell you very little about her, to be honest. She was hard-working, a stickler for detail, meticulous, but not a particularly interesting person. I know that's not a very nice thing to say, but I imagine you appreciate honesty when there's so much at stake.'

Sverrir smiled at last. 'You can say that again.' He returned to the point: 'Two doctors, then: Fridjón and Thorri. And a nurse, Elísabet.'

'Elísabet has been here a lot longer than me,' Tinna said. 'I've nothing but good to say about her. I expect she'll take over Yrsa's job.'

'How do you feel about that?'

'I haven't given it much thought. I just took it for granted. Elísabet's pretty competent, in my opinion.'

And, yes, Tinna reflected, it would certainly be an advantage to have her as boss rather than Yrsa, though she wasn't going to voice this thought aloud.

'Is it regarded as a desirable position?'

'Yrsa's, you mean?' Tinna asked, trying to buy time to consider her answer. 'Well, I suppose . . .' This time she said what was on her mind, only to regret it at once: 'Do you mean is the position desirable enough to be worth murdering someone for?'

Now it was Sverrir's turn to look a little flustered. After

a pause, he smiled and nodded: 'Er, if you want to put it like that . . .'

'I shouldn't think so. It must have been an outsider.'

'Of course, that's the most likely possibility,' Sverrir said, without much conviction.

'If not, then it must have been Broddi,' Tinna said, without really meaning anything by it. She just didn't like the idea that a doctor or a nurse could have been responsible for such a horrific crime.

'The caretaker, right? You think so? Why?'

'Why him?' She hesitated. 'Er, I don't really know, but . . . but he has keys to the building, and . . .'

'. . . and he's only a caretaker,' Sverrir finished for her.

Tinna lowered her eyes, trying to fight back the flush she could feel rising to her cheeks. 'I didn't mean it like that. I just don't know him very well. He's been here for years, like Fridjón, though not quite as long, I don't think. He's the quiet, retiring type . . .' She paused, then said: 'Look, all I meant was that it might be best to start by talking to him.'

'Of course, I'll be talking to all of you, Broddi included.' Sverrir smiled.

Tinna felt a knot forming in her stomach. A sign of guilt, perhaps, because she suddenly had a nasty feeling that she might have got Broddi into hot water with her thoughtless comments.

2012

Broddi

Broddi had made coffee, the old-fashioned way. He hadn't wanted to move over to one of those new-fangled coffee machines, which were automatic but looked so fiddly. He'd seen that kind of machine at his friends' houses, but they weren't for him. Good, old-fashioned filter coffee was all that would be on offer for the young man who had announced his visit. Coffee, yes, and a Danish pastry too. Broddi had strolled over to the bakery in honour of the occasion. Not that there was much worth having at his local bakery. He suspected that many of the pastries weren't even baked on the premises but bought in frozen and defrosted in the morning. So many changes – nothing was like it used to be. Apart from the coffee, of course.

He was getting on as well. He'd always been an old soul, but now he was seventy-six and his body was beginning to let him down. He was still pretty fit, though, in spite of his age.

It was nine years since his wife had died. As it happened, the young man, Helgi, had rung on the anniversary of her death. No doubt – of course – it had been pure coincidence, but perhaps that was why Broddi had reacted to his request better than he would have done otherwise. Normally, he preferred not to talk about what had happened up north all those years ago, but on the day Helgi called, Broddi had been feeling lonely, missing his wife so acutely that he had decided on an impulse to invite the young man round.

His wife had fallen ill and been informed by the doctors that nothing could be done; the disease was incurable and she only had a few months left to live. Understandably, the news had been a devastating blow for them both. She had sunk almost immediately into depression, whereas Broddi had tried not to lose heart and set about making plans for the time they had left together, trying to organize memorable things for them to do. But she wouldn't hear of it. One cold winter's morning not long afterwards, he had found her in the garage. She had given up during the night, gone down to the garage, got in the car and said goodbye to this life once and for all. He knew it must have been a release for her, because her illness would almost certainly have caused her suffering to the bitter end. To some extent he'd understood her, but in the immediate aftermath his overriding emotion had been anger. He hadn't even had a chance to say a proper goodbye to her. Afterwards, grief had taken over, and now, nine years later, that feeling was still dominant. He'd been left alone in the world, as they had no children.

Much to the astonishment of many, he'd decided not to sell the old white estate car she had died in. Instead, he'd kept it, and was still driving around in it today. In some strange way he felt he could sense his wife's presence in the car, and this gave him comfort, although it had been the scene and instrument of her suicide. On the other hand, he had moved out of their small bungalow, selling it and their garage, and with the proceeds of the sale he had purchased himself a modest flat on the third floor of an old apartment block in the west end of Reykjavík.

He and his wife had met relatively late in life, at around fifty, and it had always been just the two of them, but in this woman Broddi had at last found a soulmate. They had lived in the northern town of Akureyri for their first few years together, but then she had been offered a job down south and he had decided to accompany her to Reykjavík, as he was fifty-five and having trouble finding work. He'd never got himself an education. And he still felt like a marked man in Akureyri.

Helgi, the young fellow who was on his way round, had been a bit vague over the phone, though he'd explained that he was writing a Master's dissertation about the deaths at the sanatorium. He had assured Broddi that anything he said would be used strictly for his research; it wouldn't find its way into the press. A dissertation on criminology, he'd said. Criminology – they had degrees in everything nowadays.

The doorbell rang, a little out of tune since it was past its prime, like so many other things in the flat. Broddi got up from his chair in the kitchen and answered the entryphone.

'Helgi Reykdal here, to see Broddi.' The words were hard to make out, distorted by the crackling of the intercom.

'Come on up, I'm on the third floor.'

Broddi was waiting in the doorway when Helgi appeared round the corner, panting slightly after climbing all those stairs. There was no lift in this old block, which meant that sooner or later Broddi would be forced to find somewhere else to live.

'Hello, I'm Helgi.' The newcomer extended a hand. He was a little shorter than Broddi had expected from his strong, confident voice. He had black hair and a neat beard, and must be thirty, at a guess – give or take a year or two.

So that's what criminologists look like, Broddi thought, inviting him into the sitting room.

The Danish pastry was on the table and the coffee was ready in the kitchen. Broddi fetched the jug and poured a cup for his guest, then for himself, offering milk and sugar, but Helgi said he took it black.

'So, you're writing a dissertation, you say?' Broddi began, after a brief silence.

'Yes, my final project. For my Master's degree in the UK.'

'In criminology?'

'That's right.'

'Quite a lot's been written in this flat, you know,' Broddi said. 'It was home to a famous author for many years. He lived here alone, like me.'

'Oh, really?' Helgi said politely.

'Anyway, what's your interest in the deaths at the sanatorium?'

'It was an unusual case. Unusually brutal,' Helgi said.

Broddi nodded.

Helgi continued: 'And unsolved, which makes it all the more interesting.'

'Was it?' Broddi asked.

'I'm sorry? What do you mean?'

'Was it unsolved? I thought most people had joined the dots, and, well, taken it as a kind of confession, when—'

Helgi cut in before he could finish: 'A kind of confession? Interesting that you put it like that. Of course, there's no way the police could build a case on *that*, not really.'

'But didn't they close the case shortly afterwards?' Broddi asked. 'That suggests the police must have been fairly satisfied.'

Helgi nodded. 'The police can make mistakes.'

Broddi took a sip of coffee, then asked: 'You have your own pet theory then, do you? Don't tell me you're seriously hoping to solve the mystery now – what – thirty years later?'

Broddi didn't actually want to drive his visitor away, when they'd only just started chatting, but he couldn't resist needling him a bit. The coffee was still hot and the Danish pastry on the table untouched as yet.

Helgi didn't seem wrong-footed, however.

'That's not the idea at all.' He smiled. 'I think there's enough material to engage with on this case without trying to do the police's job for them. Besides, as you say, it's too long ago.'

'Yes,' Broddi agreed. 'Still, I hope I can help you in some way. Though, of course, I don't remember all the details any more.'

'Before we get on to the facts of the case . . .' Helgi paused.

The language he used was so formal that it gave Broddi a momentary flashback, the feeling that he was involved in a police interview rather than a friendly chat over coffee. Yet the young man facing him was only a student – of criminology, admittedly – not a police officer.

Helgi continued: 'I've been looking for information about the staff at the sanatorium, the names mentioned in the police reports, the people who worked with you . . . They're all still alive, aren't they?'

'Am I the first person you've spoken to?' Broddi asked in reply.

Helgi nodded. 'Yes,' he confirmed, after another brief pause.

'How come?'

'Well, for various reasons. For one thing, you live in Reykjavík . . .'

'Yes, like Tinna.'

'Yes, quite, like Tinna. I'd gathered that she lives in town too.'

'That's right.'

'Are you still friends or in contact at all these days?'

'I wouldn't really say that, but we're aware of each other's existence.'

'Do you have her phone number? It's not in the directory.'

Broddi didn't immediately answer. It occurred to him that Tinna might not want to make herself available to this man. He wondered whether he should lie to protect her; claim he didn't have her number. Then again, he felt the urge to show off a bit and prove to this young man that he had something to contribute. The upshot was that he got to his feet, fetched his old mobile phone and read out Tinna's number.

'Thanks. Then hopefully I'll be able to get hold of her at last.'

'Various reasons, you said?' Broddi prompted him, after a moment's silence.

Helgi made a puzzled noise.

'You mentioned that there were various reasons why you got in touch with me before the others, including the fact I live in Reykjavík. Was there anything else behind your decision?' he asked, though he reckoned he already knew the answer.

'Well . . . I thought it might be interesting to talk to you in light of the way, er, the way you were treated at the time. The way my colleagues . . .'

'Your colleagues?' Broddi echoed.

'I mean . . . the police . . .' Helgi replied, sounding a little unsure of himself.

'I thought you were a student,' Broddi said, trying not to let his irritation show.

'What? Oh, sure, I'm a student. But I've temped for the police in the past – that's what made me interested in criminology.'

Broddi nodded but didn't say anything for a moment

or two. 'Anyway, what do you want to know?' he asked eventually.

'Well, I thought it would be interesting to hear your side of the story. Whether you have any theories about what really happened . . .'

'Yrsa was murdered, that's a fact, and we know who did it too,' Broddi said flatly. 'But, to be honest, I don't suppose we'll ever know the reason for the killing. There were no clues then and there certainly aren't any now, all these years later.'

Helgi's face grew thoughtful and he sat forwards, as if about to speak, then leaned back again, before finally saying: 'So the police initially cocked up by arresting the wrong man, but they succeeded in solving the case satisfactorily in the end, is that it?'

Broddi let out a deep, genuine laugh: 'Solving the case? Damn it, no, the case solved itself – the police had nothing to do with it. Though they realized in the end, like everyone else, that the case was closed. That officer, Sverrir, was responsible for the cock-up. He was totally bloody useless. He was just lucky the answer landed in his lap like that. I bet he got a pat on the back, though, didn't he? Oh, I can well believe that.'

'I'm not sure, to be honest,' Helgi said.

'Not sure about what?' Broddi asked.

'I'm not sure it was a satisfactory closure, but, like I say, my aim isn't necessarily to get to the bottom of the mystery. My dissertation is more concerned with the investigation itself and how it was conducted.'

Broddi nodded, then smiled grimly. 'Well, I don't

want to get involved. I experienced it first hand, in a way that was all too personal, so as far as I'm concerned, the case was closed long ago. It's never even crossed my mind that anyone else could have done that to Yrsa; it's unthinkable.'

'Are you referring to the people who worked with her?'

'What? Yes, I suppose so. I believe the police looked into the possibility – that an outsider could have been involved, I mean – but that was just as much of a long shot.'

'It sounds as if I won't be hearing any suggestions of other possible killers from you, then?'

'Definitely not.'

'What kind of person was Yrsa?'

Broddi wasn't prepared for this question. He thought for a moment or two before answering. 'I'd known her a very long time. She'd been working at the sanatorium even longer than me. So . . .' He hesitated. 'I'd known her a long time, like I said, but I didn't know her at all well. I don't think anyone knew Yrsa well. She was a hard worker, came in early and went home late and was always willing to do overtime, as far as I can remember. I'm not aware that she ever made any enemies, but then, you know, she didn't make any friends either.'

'And the brutal mistreatment – torture, in fact – did you never wonder what the motive could have been for that? Nothing came to light during the investigation.'

Broddi shook his head. 'Of course, I wondered about that – it would be surprising if I hadn't – but I didn't see the body myself. It was only poor Tinna who had to go through that nightmare. The description was shocking enough. But I've never been able to come up with any rational explanation for it – I mean, there aren't any rational explanations for something like that.'

'What about Fridjón?' Helgi asked.

'Fridjón?'

'Can you tell me anything about him?'

'There's not much to tell. He was the director. He started working there before me and ran the place for decades. No one dared stand up to him.'

'Was he a good doctor?'

'Good? I don't know if it's my place to judge, to be honest. I expect he knew what he was doing; I don't have any reason to think otherwise.'

'What about Thorri? He's still working as a doctor, isn't he?'

'He's mainly based up north, from what I've heard,' Broddi said. 'I haven't seen him for donkey's years. He was the one who got rid of me, as you've no doubt heard.'

'No, I hadn't heard that,' Helgi replied, and Broddi realized that of course Helgi couldn't have known anything about it. It wasn't as if staffing issues at the sanatorium had been of any interest to the newspapers after the case was closed. The caretaker was simply pushed out into the cold and no one cared.

'Well, he didn't want me there any longer.'

'Any idea why?'

'It's pretty obvious, don't you think?'

Helgi didn't immediately answer, then said: 'Won't you tell me what happened?'

'It was because I was arrested and held in custody, of course. He used some other excuse but, basically, everything changed after my arrest. It's hard to clear your name in a . . . well, in a town that small.'

Broddi felt his eyes pricking with tears and blinked, struggling to hold them back. He mustn't show weakness like this. It was too shaming.

'Broddi . . .' Again, Helgi leaned forwards. 'Broddi, would you mind telling me about it, about your time in custody, I mean?' His voice was gentle and encouraging.

Broddi got abruptly to his feet. 'I'm sorry, but I have no interest in talking about it. In fact, I've got to run. There's somebody I need to see – I'd forgotten. It was nice meeting you, Helgi.'

1983

Tinna

Tinna hadn't expected to have to speak to the police again so soon. Of course, she was an important witness, she realized that, and she had to admit that she was rather enjoying her new-found status. Everyone was being so kind to her these days, asking her if it hadn't been a dreadful shock and whether there was anything they could do to make her life easier. Then there were those who just wanted to hear an eyewitness account of what she'd seen. Sometimes she obliged, though 'strictly between us', as the police had forbidden her to talk about the case while the investigation was still going on. Although she was careful not to reveal everything, she did get a secret kick out of telling people about the amputated thumb and finger lying on the bloodstained desk. These were exactly the kinds of gory details her friends were after, and suddenly she had a whole lot more 'friends' than before. Deep down, she knew she was probably just scared and that her light-hearted take was a form of defence mechanism. Her colleague had been brutally murdered and the killer was not only still out there but might actually be one of the people she worked with. Following the post-mortem, the police had broken the news to the sanatorium staff that Yrsa had died of asphyxiation as a result of pressure applied to her windpipe, but the fact she had been mutilated had not been made public.

This time, Tinna had been asked to go in to the police station in Akureyri. They had phoned the hospital at midday, so she had requested permission to pop away from work to assist with the inquiry, as she put it.

Tinna had stopped off at home before going to the station, as it wasn't far out of her way, and changed into a rather more fetching coat. She hadn't seen Sverrir since she gave him her statement and was quite looking forward to meeting him again. There had been a definite frisson between them, and she was determined to do something about it before he returned to Reykjavík. It was fine by her if the investigation didn't finish immediately, though of course it was uncomfortable having it hanging over her like a shadow. Still, she was sure that no one in their right mind would imagine that she herself could have been responsible for such a horrific crime.

At the police station Tinna was shown into an office, where, to her dismay, it wasn't Sverrir sitting behind the desk but a woman she'd never seen before. Tinna hesitated, hovering in the doorway in the faint hope that one of them was in the wrong place.

'I'm sorry, but I was supposed to be meeting Sverrir,

from CID,' Tinna said eventually, in a firm voice. She was used to standing up for her rights.

The woman stayed where she was but her mouth spread in an inscrutable smile.

'Sverrir's busy, so you're stuck with me, I'm afraid. Please, take a seat.'

Tinna obeyed reluctantly, brushing some imaginary fluff off the pretty white coat that it seemed she wouldn't get a chance to show off to Sverrir this time.

The woman held out her hand. 'Hello, I'm Hulda,' she said. 'Hulda Hermannsdóttir. I'm from CID too.'

Hulda was noticeably older than Sverrir, probably getting on for forty – the very thought of being that old filled Tinna with horror – so that must mean she was senior to him.

'Oh, hello, nice to meet you. Sorry, it's just that I was expecting to see Sverrir.' Then Tinna added ingratiatingly: 'I assume he must work for you?' She hoped this would put her in the woman's good books.

But Hulda looked a little disconcerted. She dropped her gaze to the papers on her desk and it appeared for a moment as if she wasn't going to answer, then she mumbled: 'Actually, Sverrir's in charge of this investigation. I came up from Reykjavík with him to . . . to assist.'

Tinna thought she detected a note of bitterness in the woman's voice.

'Oh,' she said. 'I see.'

'I've been over his report of your conversation following your discovery of the victim,' Hulda continued, rather stiffly. 'If I've understood Sverrir right, you had your own theory that the caretaker, Broddi, might have been responsible for the murder.'

Tinna hadn't been prepared for this. 'Well, I . . . er, I might have implied that. To be honest, I just thought he was the most likely suspect.'

'Did you have any particular reason to think so?'

'No, I wouldn't say that but, er, you know, it was a vicious attack, absolutely shocking. And I can't imagine many people would be capable of doing something like that.'

'So you decided to point us towards Broddi.'

'Er, that's probably putting it too strongly. I just thought it would be natural to take a particularly good look at him.' Tinna had dug herself into this hole and now she would have to do her best to claw her way out again. She felt a stab of guilt as she pictured Broddi, that nice man who was always so willing to help her. How could she have accused him so thoughtlessly? But it was too late to take it back now.

'Sverrir's going to question him in more depth today,' Hulda said, after a brief silence. 'So we just wanted to get this straight with you.'

'Yes, er, that's all there is to it, really. Anyway, is that everything?' Tinna prepared to stand up.

'Not quite, Tinna, not quite. A vicious attack, that was how you described it just now, wasn't it?'

'Mm? Oh. Yes. You can't really call it anything else when someone goes around cutting people's fingers off.'

'Quite. You are aware that this information is to be kept strictly confidential, aren't you?'

It was then that it dawned on Tinna what this meeting was really about. She felt herself breaking out in a sweat and her heart began to pound.

She nodded. 'Yes, of course.'

'Have you discussed it with anyone else, Tinna?'

She didn't immediately answer, then said: 'Well, it's come up in conversation. You know how it is.'

'Have you told anyone what you saw?' Hulda was watching her with an uncomfortably penetrating gaze. Tinna got the feeling this woman was razor sharp and that it would be a bad idea to make an enemy of her. It almost certainly wouldn't be a good idea to lie to her either.

'Well, I may have mentioned it to one or two friends of mine, in complete confidence, of course. Has somebody said something?'

Hulda was silent for a long moment, her eyes fixed on Tinna, whose discomfort was growing with every second that passed.

'Yes, we got wind of that, I'm afraid. I just wanted to stress to you, Tinna, that this case is extremely sensitive. I don't believe you'd want to do anything to compromise such a serious investigation, would you?'

'No, no, of course not,' Tinna replied, hoping that this would be enough to let her off the hook for now and that her slip-up wouldn't have any further repercussions.

Hulda rose to her feet.

'Excellent, Tinna, excellent,' she said. 'It was nice meeting you. I hope you've recovered from the shock.'

Tinna nodded and stood up as well. As she left the room, she almost walked slap bang into Sverrir.

'Hello again,' he said politely. And this time she was sure there was a spark in his eyes, a hint of mutual interest.

'Oh, hello, nice to see you again,' she said shyly. She didn't usually react like this, but there was something about the man that made her self-conscious.

He glanced at Hulda, then back at Tinna. 'Everything's fine, isn't it?'

Tinna couldn't work out whether the question was addressed to her or to Hulda, but it was clear that he was aware of the reason for their meeting, which was only to be expected, given that Hulda worked for him. Tinna nodded, afraid that she must look rather sheepish.

'Good,' he said, meeting Tinna's gaze for a moment with an expression that was hard to read. Then he turned back to Hulda: 'Hulda, your daughter's been calling again, asking for you.' From his tone it was plain that he had little patience with personal phone calls at work.

'Oh, right,' Hulda said. 'I'll call her back.'

Tinna took the opportunity to slip out without saying goodbye.

2012

Helgi

It was past seven in the evening. Helgi had gone to a café after his meeting with Broddi, taking along the Peter Duluth novel, which he finished over coffee. Deciding to eat supper there too, he ordered a club sandwich with chips and lingered over his meal, enjoying the chance to relax. He hadn't heard from Bergthóra or made any effort to get hold of her. They tended to avoid each other after one of their explosive rows, which had unfortunately become increasingly frequent over the years. Sometimes he allowed himself to wonder whether they might have reached the end of the road, but neither of them had put this possibility into words, at least not in any seriousness. Deep down he felt utterly demoralized about the state of their relationship.

Helgi didn't immediately get up and leave, despite having finished his book and his meal some time ago. He had been thinking back over his conversation with Broddi and was having trouble working the man out. Granted, it must be difficult for him to talk about what had happened to him, especially as he had been the only person arrested as a suspect. He'd been held in custody and forced to watch his name dragged through the mud by the press. Helgi had done his best to trawl through all the newspaper archives before starting work on his dissertation, and it was evident from what he'd read that the press had gone to town on the poor guy. He was the perfect scapegoat, as far as Helgi could see; the only person working at the hospital who could have been regarded as an outsider. The medical staff had watched each other's backs, but no one had bothered about the caretaker, though he had worked there longer than most. Back in the days when the highly infectious disease had claimed so many lives, it must have taken real courage and resilience, Helgi reflected, to work at the sanatorium, regardless of whether you were a doctor, a nurse or a caretaker. He had done some background reading about the period but couldn't really imagine what conditions would have been like.

Helgi's main interest in talking to Broddi had been to get an insight into the time he'd spent in custody and the impact the experience had had on him. That would have been a story worth hearing, but it would have to wait – for the moment, at least. Helgi hadn't entirely given up hope that he'd be able to persuade the old caretaker to open up. But, for now, the next thing on his agenda was to see if Tinna would agree to having a chat with him.

His phone rang. It was Bergthóra.

Helgi was about to answer, but at the last second he

changed his mind and got to his feet. It was time to kiss and make up after yesterday's fight, and it would be better to have that conversation in person, since their reconciliations more often than not ended up in bed. He paid and hurried outside into the dusk. There was a definite hint of spring in the air but it was still bitterly cold. He hadn't dressed warmly enough and now regretted not having put on his down jacket, but that would have been a mark of surrender, an admission that the Icelandic spring was no more than an illusion, no more than winter in fancy dress.

2012

Helgi

The conversation with Bergthóra had not ended with a happy reconciliation in bed. It hadn't developed into a screaming row like the previous evening, thank God, as he didn't want another visit from the boys in blue, but peace had not been restored. The quarrel would just have to be allowed to run its course. At times, when all was sweetness and light between them, they discussed the possibility of having children; both wanted a family, but they kept putting it off because they were too busy with their work or studies. But the very idea was becoming increasingly absurd these days, with their relationship in tatters.

Helgi sent up a silent prayer that the police officers who came round hadn't gossiped about the call-out to their colleagues, because, if they had, he feared the news would quickly reach the ears of Magnús, the departmental head who was so keen to have him on board.

For now, though, it looked as if Helgi would be sleeping on the sofa for the second night in a row. Bergthóra had retired to bed, although it was only just gone nine, and he had the whole evening ahead of him.

Was it too late to call Tinna? It would be great if he could make an appointment to see her and get his dissertation moving again. Then he'd sit down at the computer and do a bit more work before rewarding himself by choosing another paperback from his classic crime collection.

He dialled the number before he had a chance to get cold feet. Acting on impulse was often the best way to get things done.

The phone rang and rang. Helgi was about to give up all hope that it would be answered when a voice said: 'Yes, hello?' A female voice, in a questioning or puzzled tone, as if the woman was being cautious because she didn't recognize the caller's number.

'Is that Tinna Einarsdóttir?'

'Yes, it is,' she said, still sounding a little suspicious.

'I'm sorry to disturb you so late. My name's Helgi.' He wanted to add that he was calling from the police, but of course that would be misleading. 'I got your number from Broddi – you remember him, don't you?'

There was a short delay before she answered: 'Broddi? Er, yes, I know who he is. What do you want?'

'Nothing particularly urgent. It's just that I'm writing an MA dissertation about the events at the sanatorium in 1983, the deaths—'

He got no further: she had hung up.

Hell.

He was getting nowhere fast. First, he'd hit a brick wall in his conversation with Broddi; now Tinna wouldn't even talk to him. Luckily, he'd already made a good start on his dissertation, largely by slogging through the old records, but his interviews with the people involved were supposed to have been the backbone of his study and – no less important – they were the main reason why his tutor had agreed to his unusual subject matter.

On reflection, Helgi found Broddi and Tinna's reactions rather odd. Of course, you couldn't expect people to take much pleasure in raking up traumatic events from the past, but he hadn't been prepared for them to stonewall him like this.

In fact, their behaviour had begun to ring warning bells, giving him that gut feeling he'd sometimes experienced when he was working for the police – a hunch that they might have something to hide. Was it possible that he was being handed an opportunity to solve a cold case?

To distract himself from these thoughts, he went over to the bookcase.

The shelves reached from floor to ceiling, a whole wall of books, mainly crime novels, consisting of his father's library and his own collection. They were a constant source of friction between him and Bergthóra. No reader herself, she complained that they took up far too much space, and she was particularly unimpressed by the tatty Icelandic paperbacks. During one of their quarrels, she had referred to them as worthless junk. And maybe they weren't worth anything in the conventional sense, but it was hard to put a price on a collection like this. Practically a complete set of all the translated crime novels from the years when first his grandfather, then his father, ran the bookshop – until the day when his father had collapsed, surrounded by the old volumes. A customer had found him, but by then it was too late. The doctor thought he'd probably had a heart attack an hour or so earlier and that it might have been possible to save him if he'd been discovered sooner.

That had left the problem of what to do with the bookshop. Helgi's mother, who was nearing retirement age, hadn't been particularly keen on the idea of serving in the shop and, besides, she had her own interests. And Helgi, their only child, couldn't face making a career of it either. By then he had moved south to go to university in Reykjavík and met Bergthóra, so he had no desire to move back to Akureyri, despite his love for the books.

It had fallen to him to stay on in the town for several days after the funeral to go through the stock, choosing the titles he wanted to keep from the shop and from his father's private library. This had been easier said than done, but the classic crime novels had been the first on his list. After that, he'd had the shop valued, including the contents of the warehouse, the business and the small commercial premises that his father had owned outright after running it for so many years. It had taken a while to find a buyer. Plenty of people had expressed interest in the premises but not in the books, but Helgi had been determined, if possible, to pass on the business and property as a unit to someone who would be interested in running it as a bookshop. He'd succeeded in the end. The place had been bought by a middle-aged widow. Her offer had been lower than several others, but although neither Helgi nor his mother were well off, he'd permitted himself this indulgence on behalf of them both, to sell the business for less than it was worth in order to preserve his father's and grandfather's legacy, at least for a little while longer. His mother still lived up north and was in good health, working for the local council. He knew he took her for granted, that he wasn't dutiful enough about visiting her, though she had twice travelled to see him and Bergthóra in the UK and now made regular trips to Reykjavík.

Helgi thought with a sudden rush of nostalgia about his little home town on the fjord, so different from the urban sprawl of Reykjavík. He supposed he'd always regarded the capital as a temporary staging post rather than a permanent home. Akureyri, surrounded by green mountains in summer and snow-capped peaks in winter, seemed a much more romantic place to him. Despite its northern latitude, it had a much pleasanter climate; the summers were sunnier, the winters more Christmassy. And although Reykjavík now struck him as small after his time in the UK, in comparison Akureyri had the intimacy of a village. It felt as if everyone there knew each other and took pride in their town.

Returning to the present, he started taking books off the shelves, one after the other, and cradling them in his hands. He'd put the Peter Duluth novel back in its place beside an old title by one of his favourite authors, Ellery Queen. Queen hadn't been one but two people, the cousins Frederic Dannay and Manfred Lee. Helgi had been particularly taken with the first books in their series, classic American mysteries, featuring a protagonist with the same name as the authors' pseudonym, Ellery Queen.

Such was Helgi's enthusiasm that in his free time he had actually translated the first book, *The Roman Hat Mystery*, which came out in 1929, into Icelandic. It had taken him two years, but he still hadn't found the courage to submit it to a publisher. He had no idea how easy it would be to acquire the translation rights to the novel, but it was still his dream to have it published. He had embarked on the translation after his father died, motivated perhaps in part by guilt at his decision not to keep the bookshop going himself. Translation was Helgi's way of making a contribution to the world of detective fiction that he and his father had both held in such high regard.

He loved the intellectual puzzles the books contained, the tidiness of the mysteries and their solutions in contrast to the messiness of real life. And their evocation of the past too. He couldn't help reflecting on the blandness of modern office life in the police compared to the glamour of walking around in a hat and trench coat like the detectives in his novels. Pure escapism, of course.

His favourite Ellery Queen novel, and the only title available in Icelandic, *The Dutch Shoe Mystery*, was truly one of the best. The Icelandic translation had been published in Akureyri in 1945, and this connection with their hometown was probably why it had always occupied a special place in his and his father's collection. Helgi could still remember when and where he had first read it. He'd had the day off school, in the depths of winter – he must have been twelve or thirteen years old at the time – and settled down on the floor in a corner at the back of the bookshop, completely absorbed by the story. Although the title hadn't aged that well in comparison to some of its contemporaries, Helgi still got a warm feeling when he took it down from the shelf. He was a boy again, and all his problems temporarily receded into the background; even the aftershock of his latest fight with Bergthóra grew remote and hazy, as if he hadn't actually taken part in it himself.

That was exactly the feeling he was after now. A flight from reality.

Taking *The Dutch Shoe Mystery* from the shelf, he settled down on the floor in the corner and began to read.

1983

Tinna

Tinna lay in bed in her small flat, not far from the grammar school where she had taken her leaving exams back in the day. She had bought the flat, with help from her parents, in a bid for independence, though her family home wasn't exactly far away; it was only in the next street. She knew there was a hot evening meal waiting for her there whenever she wanted.

It was three in the morning. Tinna had slept for an hour or so before being woken by a bad dream.

She had talked matter-of-factly about her discovery of the body, telling the story as though nothing could be more natural, as though she were describing a scene from a film rather than real events. She'd pretended it hadn't affected her and that she was impervious to the shock, but as soon as night fell, things took on a very different appearance. The moment she shut her eyes, she was confronted by the image of Yrsa's body, and sleep stubbornly refused to come. When it did finally relent, her dreams kept turning into nightmares. The horrifying expression on the dead woman's face, the dark pool of blood on the desk by the black telephone, the small radio and inkwell – everything she had witnessed would intensify into a black-and-white nightmare. Then she would wake up in the early hours like now, drenched in sweat.

She knew she wouldn't be able to get back to sleep. That she'd turn up to work feeling shattered, yet again. Things couldn't go on like this. To make matters worse, she would have to face them all – the people she worked with. She felt uneasy in their company, uneasy in the corridors of the hospital, as if the threat were still hanging over them; in fact, she was sure it wasn't over yet. Perhaps she was just being paranoid, but Yrsa's death had felt like a beginning, not an end. More than anything, though, she was afraid of Broddi. Up to now she had liked him fine and chatted to him companionably when they were alone together in the wing in the evenings. She'd even felt sorry for him, because his family had been directly affected by tuberculosis. He had his own connection to the history of the dreaded disease that the sanatorium staff had once battled so heroically.

Now, though, she could feel her flesh creeping in Broddi's presence. He was responsible for all kinds of odd jobs at the hospital, which meant he was there on the premises day in, day out, and he'd done nothing to change this habit since Yrsa's death – indeed he had no good reason to. But Tinna was starting to believe her own theory that Broddi must be the killer. Either Broddi or some outsider. For some reason she found it more reassuring if she could endow the invisible menace with a face, and her choice had fallen on the caretaker. The look in his eyes, which she had previously interpreted as friendly, now seemed sinister to her; his affable greetings in the corridors of the hospital struck her as cold and devoid of feeling.

She kept telling herself that her fear was irrational, something she'd invented, completely baseless, but then she would sense the trepidation mounting inside her again and convince herself that Broddi needed to be taken out of circulation, or whatever the phrase was, so the police could investigate him properly. Establish his guilt or innocence once and for all.

She tried to hide her apprehension, though she must have seemed less chatty around him than she used to be. But then nothing was as it used to be at the sanatorium; all the staff's interaction seemed stilted and constrained these days.

As a rule, Tinna avoided entering the old hospital wards if possible as she found the atmosphere there macabre; there were reminders of death in every corner, and the narrow corridors seemed eerie and oppressive.

But the ghosts of the long-dead patients were forced to take a back seat now, because it was the chilling memory of what had happened to Yrsa that held everyone in its grip.

2012

Helgi

'Helgi! Magnús here. Is this a good moment?'

The voice seemed to smarm into his ear. Helgi had talked to Magnús several times over the phone but only once met him in person. He reminded himself that this man would soon be his boss if things continued the way they were going. The job couldn't be faulted; in fact, it was one of the best available to Helgi in Iceland, but, if he were honest, he didn't really take to Magnús himself. It was hard to put a finger on what precisely had given rise to his slight feeling of antipathy, beyond the sense that there was something fake or superficial about the man's manner.

'Hello, no, it's fine, all good. How are you?'

'I just wanted to find out when you could start. We're keen to have you on the team, Helgi.'

'Yes, well, I'm still finishing my MA dissertation. So, this summer or autumn, I suppose.' As Helgi said this, he could feel his dream of working abroad slipping through his fingers.

It was the same sensation he'd had when he moved back to Iceland after his studies; an instinct warning him that he shouldn't be going home. When he landed at Keflavík, it had felt as if a door was closing, as if he had abandoned the opportunity of a lifetime.

Now he was committing himself to Iceland for the foreseeable future, and the thought gave him a pang. He mustn't show ingratitude; he was lucky to be sought after and he knew that many people would have killed to be in his shoes. There was no plan to advertise the position, Magnús had explained; they were keeping it open for him.

'Well, the sooner the better, Helgi. You know, we can give you a bit of leeway to work on your dissertation alongside your job to begin with. It's really not a problem.'

'OK, I'll give it some thought.' The prospect wasn't a bad one: it would break up the monotony of writing and, above all, get him out of the house, which would help him stay sane and keep his relationship with Bergthóra going. 'How much notice do you need?'

'Notice? None, actually. We can sort things out as soon as you decide you want to start. We've got an older woman here who's well past her sell-by date. She's due to retire later this year in any case, so I'm sure she'll be only too happy to be released a bit sooner. You know what it's like when people have reached that stage; their office full of junk, old files and ghosts of the past. To be honest, it would be a kindness to let her go early.'

'Right, OK, I get you. I'll give it some serious thought, I promise. I'll be in touch shortly.'

'I look forward to it, Helgi.'

1983

Elísabet

Elísabet had ended up in Akureyri by chance. She had grown up in Reykjavík and had expected to make a life for herself there, but then she had met her dream prince, who had lured her up north.

They were still married, she and the one-time dream prince, though their relationship had long ago soured, no trace of romance remained, and their son was the only thing keeping them together. He was five years old and since, for his sake, Elísabet couldn't abandon her marriage, she struggled on with it, hoping that things would get better. Despite her certainty that she and her husband wouldn't be together for the rest of their lives, she had decided to give their marriage another ten years, just until their son reached his teens. Fifteen years, max. Life wasn't all bad; she had an interesting job and had made friends up north, it was just that she had no love left for her husband. Every now and then she managed to get away for a short break, visiting friends in other parts of the country, and at those times she would indulge in regrets about the kind of life she could have had if she had never met this man, fallen in love and married him in a moment of madness.

After work, she liked to relax in front of the TV; her greatest pleasure was settling down on a Wednesday evening to watch the latest antics of JR Ewing and co. in *Dallas*. And the other day a new series, *Philip Marlowe, Private Eye*, had begun, which looked very promising. Apart from that, she passed the time by reading. Some years ago her friends had tried to get her interested in skiing. 'It's such a waste living here if you don't ski,' they had said, and she'd given it a try, even attended a couple of courses, but it wasn't for her; she simply wasn't the outdoors type. She was happiest at work.

Or rather, she *used to be* happiest at work, before everything changed.

The impact of Yrsa's death on the sanatorium staff had been shattering. They barely spoke to one another these days but walked the corridors in silence, except when the subject of Yrsa came up. Tinna was by far the worst in that respect, constantly gossiping and spreading stories. To begin with, Elísabet had got on well with the young woman, who'd come across as promising and conscientious, but now Tinna seemed determined to milk the fact that she had found Yrsa's body for all it was worth, wallowing in being the centre of attention. Her behaviour struck Elísabet as inappropriate, to say the least.

There was a cloud hanging over every member of staff, and things couldn't go on like this for ever.

The police were being tight-lipped about the progress of the inquiry, and in the absence of information, rumours flourished. Yrsa's body had been found in her office, deep inside the building, too far from the front door for it to be plausible that she could have heard someone knocking and let them in. There was only one entrance and no doorbell. The only way of entering the building outside office hours was with a key, unless her killer had made an appointment to see her. Of course, that possibility couldn't be ruled out, but it was fairly obvious that the police were focusing all their attention on the people who had keys. It was a select group: Elísabet herself, of course; the director, Fridjón; the houseman, Thorri; Tinna; and, last but not least, Broddi.

It hadn't escaped Elísabet that the police were showing an increasing interest in Broddi. That could be because he was behaving suspiciously, appearing constantly on edge, or it could simply be that he was an easy target. She kept wondering if she should have a word with that young policeman, Sverrir, or maybe with Hulda, the female officer working on the investigation with him. Hulda seemed friendlier and more approachable, but it was clear from their interaction that Sverrir was in charge and that he kept his colleague on a pretty tight rein. Elísabet could have spoken to either of them to assure them that Broddi wasn't the type to commit murder; he was far too placid and unassuming. Yet she didn't do it, because the truth was that it was convenient for her – and for the others – if the poor man took the brunt of the police's attention.

No one wanted to find themselves in the spotlight of a murder inquiry.

1983

Tinna

The sun had put in an appearance that morning, raising Tinna's spirits as she drove to work. The journey was so much more enjoyable on a beautiful day like this, the valley green, the sky an intense blue, the hospital buildings as brilliantly white as the snow on the mountaintops. She hoped her good mood would last, though the atmosphere at the sanatorium was dreary beyond belief, enough to dampen anyone's spirits. If only the police would hurry up and solve the crime, so life at work could go back to how it used to be. Five days had passed since Yrsa's death and there was still no sign that they had made any real progress, despite the continuing presence in Akureyri of Sverrir and Hulda, the detectives from Reykjavík.

The director, Fridjón, had done little to try and boost morale among his staff, apart from holding one short meeting the day after the body was discovered. But he had seemed so devastated himself that he could do little to put heart into his team. Since then, he had barely been seen in the corridors, and on the few occasions Tinna had caught sight of him he had looked like a shadow of his former self.

But this wasn't the only reason why Tinna could hardly wait for the case to be closed. The moment it was, she intended to make a play for Sverrir. She'd already established that he was single, by cornering Hulda and asking her in a roundabout way.

Tinna parked in her usual space near the sanatorium and walked the last stretch.

Given the direction her thoughts had been taking, she was rather startled to see none other than Sverrir himself standing at the entrance as she approached. The police car was parked a little way off, half hidden from view behind the trees. She quickened her pace.

'Sverrir,' she called. He had already opened the door but looked round and smiled when he heard her voice, and surveyed her for a moment or two without speaking.

'Hello, Tinna,' he said at last, with unusual warmth. 'You always get in first, don't you?'

She nodded.

'I was just going to take another look at the scene, as we're still trying to build up a picture of what happened. I wasn't expecting anyone else to be here this early.'

'I'm an early bird. I usually wake up at the crack of dawn and, since I can't get back to sleep, I feel I might as well come into work instead of hanging around, drinking coffee alone at home.' She stressed the word *alone*. Then added jokily: 'And we get paid overtime too. Seeing as we have to use up our overtime allowance every month, I'd rather start the day early than stay late.'

'Same here.'

'Have you had coffee yet?' she asked once they were standing in the green-painted entrance hall. They had been greeted by the pervasive hospital smell – a smell she could never entirely become inured to, although she tended to notice it less as the day wore on.

'No, actually.' He looked round and smiled at her again.

'I'll put some on – I know just the right blend,' she said, feeling almost as if they were on a first date.

'That sounds great.'

'You mentioned Broddi the other day,' Sverrir said, once they were seated at the table in the cafeteria. A delicious aroma of coffee rose from their steaming mugs.

'Oh,' she said. 'Yes.'

'Did you have any particular reason for saying what you did?' he asked casually, and she was suddenly unsure whether this was a chat or a formal interview.

'Er, how do you mean?'

'You thought it was possible he could have been involved in Yrsa's death.' A serious note had entered Sverrir's voice.

'Ah. Yes, I did,' she admitted warily.

'Why was that?'

'Well, I thought he was behaving a bit oddly when he turned up to work that morning.' Broddi had got in shortly after Tinna, before the police arrived, but made himself scarce as soon as Tinna told him what had happened. That could be viewed as suspicious, though she supposed it was understandable too, as no one would want to be caught up in a murder investigation.

Still, she was eager to please, and it was clear from Sverrir's questions that Broddi was under suspicion. Keen as she was to see the back of this business, she'd like to be part of the solution too, by helping Sverrir solve the mystery. Working together was bound to bring them closer.

She found herself saying, out of the blue, without a shred of evidence: 'Actually, I noticed when he turned up that there was a stain on his trousers that could have been blood.' She didn't hesitate for a second – after all, it could have been true, even if it wasn't. She had a habit of telling lies, mostly about trivial things, though occasionally about more serious ones, and usually got away with it on the strength of her winsome smile. She'd done it ever since she was a child. Everyone enjoyed exaggerating their stories, she justified it to herself, and so did she; it was just that she went a step further than most. As far back as she could remember, she'd found it easy to embellish the truth, and as a child she'd often been scolded for it, but gradually she had learnt to take more care. The truth was that life was easier if you tweaked the facts a little in your favour.

'Are you serious?' At last she had Sverrir's full attention. 'Why didn't you say anything before?'

She employed her special, wide-eyed smile. 'I didn't want to get him into trouble. I like him. And I could have been mistaken – I was in such a state at the time.'

'Yes, of course, but we'll have to look into it, anyway,' Sverrir said grimly.

'I suppose I can understand that.'

She thought she'd regret the lie afterwards, as sometimes happened, but to her surprise she didn't. She remained perfectly calm. After all, it had brought her and Sverrir closer.

It occurred to her to invite him round for coffee, taking advantage of what felt like a promising spark between them, and the words were almost out of her mouth when she changed her mind at the last moment. The project had too much riding on it; she mustn't push her luck. Sverrir wasn't about to leave Akureyri any time soon, which meant she still had room for manoeuvre. The key was to wait for the murder to be solved, one way or another. It wasn't really any of her concern exactly how that was achieved.

1983

Sverrir

Sverrir wasn't exactly looking forward to what he had to do; he knew it wouldn't give him any satisfaction. As they drove up the valley in the gathering dusk, heading for the old sanatorium, he debated with himself yet again about whether he was making the right decision.

He wasn't sure, but at the end of the day, the buck stopped with him; it was his responsibility to crack the case and for that he would have to trust his own judgement. Hulda, sitting beside him in the passenger seat, remained silent. She didn't talk much at the best of times, which made her all the more effective as a listener; she was often quicker than him to grasp what was going on. She was cautious, as though she'd hit a brick wall once too often at work. Naturally, they'd discussed this next step, but she had disagreed with him. To her credit, she believed in plain speaking.

Although they were working together on the investigation, she tended to keep herself to herself in her free time, staying in her room at the guest house or going out for solitary meals. She didn't evince any desire to eat with him or go for a drink after work. Twice in the last few days he'd invited her out for a burger, despite having no real interest in getting to know her. As her boss, he felt it was his duty to spend at least part of the time with her outside working hours, so she wouldn't be left entirely to her own devices in Akureyri, but on both occasions she had declined his offer, saying she was just going to have a snack in her room. So Sverrir had made an effort to get acquainted with the local police instead, on the basis that it was a good policy to have friends and allies in as many places as possible in his line of work. His approach had paid off: working with the local boys had gone more smoothly than he'd anticipated and he felt the investigation was being conducted in a spirit of full cooperation.

He paused in the entrance hall to look at his partner: 'Do you still think I'm making a mistake, Hulda?'

She hesitated, perhaps because they had already come so far that there was no point objecting at this stage. Then she said: 'I have a feeling you are, Sverrir. In my opinion, we should hold our horses and do a bit more groundwork first.'

He smiled. His mind was made up and he was almost pleased to find that her plea for caution had no effect. It was decided. Even if something went wrong, it wouldn't be his fault. He wasn't the one who had mutilated and murdered an older woman: the responsibility for that lay squarely with the killer; the responsibility for the crime and its fall-out. All Sverrir could do was hope that they were on their way to arrest the right man.

Hulda added: 'But don't misunderstand me, Sverrir – I'm not necessarily saying we've got the wrong guy. I just have the feeling we're jumping the gun a bit.'

He appreciated Hulda's persistence. She must have realized that he wasn't going to change his mind, so she was back-pedalling slightly. He knew she was extremely sharp and didn't get the recognition she deserved but went on diligently plugging away nonetheless, with no thought of quitting. If he was honest, he doubted he'd stick his neck out to help her towards a promotion. It wasn't in his own interests – she'd have to fend for herself – but it was useful to work with her and try to learn from her, as more often than not she picked up on clues that had passed him by.

The first person they encountered in the corridors of the hospital was Tinna. Typical. But then she had given them quite a helping hand, whether she knew it or not. And she always gave him a friendly smile. Such a nice, attractive girl. Perhaps there could have been something between them, had the circumstances been different. Right now, though, he didn't have the luxury to indulge in thoughts of that kind.

Hulda got in first: 'Hello, Tinna. Is Broddi in today?'

'Er, yes, I saw him just now. He was in the cafeteria. Shall I—'

Hulda interrupted her: 'No, thanks, we'll have a look in there ourselves. We just want a word with him.'

Sverrir would have done things differently. There was no need to inform Tinna of the reason for their presence there, though he supposed it would become common knowledge before long. He loathed hospitals, couldn't stand the smell or the atmosphere, and would rather be almost anywhere else right now. Still, with any luck they were about to make a breakthrough in the case, and then he would be able to go home, back to his usual routine. It was a strain living in an unfamiliar place for days at a time. He and Hulda were putting up at a guest house in town and, although clean, his room was drab and cheerless, and the radiator didn't work properly either, so he was freezing night after night. This only made him the more eager to solve the case as quickly as possible. He'd tried to complain to the powers that be, requesting that he at least, as head of the investigation, should be moved to a proper hotel. As far as he was concerned, Hulda could stay where she was – after all, she hadn't complained.

Broddi was sitting in the cafeteria, hunched over a mug, his face grim. The room was filled with a pleasant smell of freshly brewed coffee. He didn't seem to notice their arrival. Sverrir paused in the doorway for a moment or two, Hulda waiting behind him.

Although he wasn't that old, Broddi's face was deeply lined, his hair – if it had ever been thick – was thinning now, and his whole demeanour was expressive of misery. Of course, being unhappy didn't necessarily equate to being a cold-blooded killer, but Sverrir was hoping that in this case it did. Because if the man was innocent, being arrested for murder would only deepen his woes.

'Good evening, Broddi,' Sverrir said in a voice heavy with authority, causing the caretaker to jump. Broddi glanced up, first at Sverrir, then at Hulda, as if he knew what was coming, Sverrir thought. As if his life had brought him nothing but misfortune piled on misfortune, and that nothing could surprise him any longer, except perhaps good news. But they were not here as the bearers of good news.

'We wanted—' Hulda began, but Sverrir cut her off. He wasn't about to let her steal his thunder. This was *his* investigation, *his* decision. And it would be his triumph, not hers, if things turned out well.

'Sorry, Broddi, but I'm afraid we're going to have to ask you to accompany us to the station,' he said. Even without looking over his shoulder, he could sense that Hulda was offended by the way he'd interrupted her.

Broddi didn't stir from his chair. He took a mouthful of coffee, but they could see that his hand was shaking. 'Accompany you? Why?'

'It would probably be best to save that conversation for the station, Broddi,' Sverrir said, trying to come across as calm but resolute.

'We . . . we can talk just as easily here,' Broddi objected, his voice rising.

Sverrir was afraid the other staff would hear him. He had no desire to make this any more difficult than necessary.

He took a step towards Broddi. 'It would be better to discuss this elsewhere.'

'No, I work here. I've got things to do. I haven't got time to go anywhere. I've worked here all my life and I'm not about to neglect my duties today.' In spite of his defiant words, there was a tremor in Broddi's voice.

'OK, fine. It's like this, Broddi: we have reason to believe that you were responsible for Yrsa's death.'

Broddi's expression was hard to read but, rather than surprise, his dominant emotion appeared to be anger, even fury.

'You . . . you can't . . . Why? Why me?' he spluttered, almost shouting now.

Sverrir found himself raising his voice in response: 'Because we have reasonable grounds for suspicion. I'm afraid you have no alternative but to come with us, Broddi.' The last thing Sverrir wanted was to drag the man out in handcuffs; it was bad enough having to arrest him in the first place. And he couldn't be a hundred per cent sure that he and Hulda had read the situation right. But he had no intention of backing down now; that was unthinkable. He mustn't show any sign of weakness before a suspect – or Hulda, for that matter – as the news was bound to get out and might make life difficult for him down the line.

'I'm not budging an inch,' Broddi said, his voice still shaking. 'You lot always pick on us. My mum never had a chance – all the men she knew betrayed her, including my dad, and I never even found out who he was. We were always broke. Now Mum's dead and I'm on my own, and just as I'm trying to sort out my life and make something of myself, to get back on my feet, you lot are determined to drag me down into the mud, lock me up behind bars, just because I'm an easy target – aren't you?' The words came tumbling out and he only stopped when he ran out of breath.

'Look, Broddi, I'm afraid I don't know your story, I know nothing about your past, and you have my sympathy if what you say is true, but a serious crime has been committed here and we need – well, we need you to come with us to answer a few questions.'

'What questions? And what happens if I say no? What are you going to do about it?'

Sverrir considered. After a moment's pause, he said: 'You know we can take you in by force, but we really don't want to have to do that. It would be better for everyone if you just came in to the station with us voluntarily, so we could have a proper chat there. How does that sound?'

Broddi was silent, but Sverrir thought he had calmed down slightly.

'I haven't done anything,' Broddi said. 'You know that, don't you? I haven't killed anyone.' Suddenly all the fight seemed to go out of him and he looked utterly defeated.

Sverrir nodded and glanced at Hulda, who gave the impression of wanting to say something, though the words didn't come.

'We'll discuss all this elsewhere, Broddi.' Sverrir put a wary hand on the man's arm and helped him to his feet. 'Come with us now.'

'All right, I'll come. I'll talk to you, but you're making a mistake.'

Broddi went with them, walking slowly, his head bowed.

'I'll be free to go by this evening, won't I?' he asked after a moment, hopefully.

'We'll see,' Sverrir replied, although he knew full well

that the plan was to leave Broddi to stew in the cells overnight in the hope of eliciting a confession. In fact, Sverrir planned to keep him in custody for several days. They might as well do this thing properly. He'd put his money on Broddi and he didn't want to be proved wrong.

1983

Hulda

'We can't hold him any longer, Sverrir – that's obvious, isn't it?'

Hulda wasn't in the habit of contradicting her superiors this bluntly, but she felt she didn't have a choice. They had no good evidence against Broddi.

'The custody order was clear; we've got a few more days,' Sverrir said, though he sounded uncertain.

'But what if he's innocent? Are we going to waste all our energy trying to pin a murder charge on someone whose only crime is to be a bit of a misfit? You know as well as I do, Sverrir, that we got a custody order largely because he's a sitting duck.'

Sverrir nodded. 'Maybe, but that doesn't automatically mean he's innocent.'

Perhaps she was being too shrill, Hulda thought, but she just wasn't herself at the moment. She was feeling so lonely in Akureyri, missing Jón and Dimma. Time seemed to be slipping away so fast: it was unbelievable to think that Dimma would be ten next year. Jón's business had been doing so well recently that they were planning a holiday abroad. They were such a close-knit family that only getting to talk to them once a day wasn't enough. She'd had a fight with her mother too, the day before she left, which still rankled. Hulda had dared to bring up the subject of her father, an American serviceman about whom she knew nothing and who, she guessed, was almost certainly in the dark about the fact he had a daughter in Iceland. As usual, her mother had refused to discuss it, let alone to help her trace him. Hulda sometimes felt a hollowness inside when she thought about her father; she so longed for a chance to meet him and get to know him. Of course, she could try to trace him on her own, but she couldn't bring herself to do something that was so obviously against her mother's wishes. Perhaps she would have to wait until her mother was dead before starting down that particular road.

'He's obviously suffering, Sverrir,' she said, toning down her vehemence. She'd looked in on Broddi twice in the cells and it was clear that the incarceration was affecting him badly, though he had only been there for one night. She was genuinely worried about the man.

'Yes, I know, but there's not a lot I can do about that. It goes without saying that it's not a situation anyone wants to find themselves in.' After a pause, Sverrir went on: 'You know as well as I do, Hulda, that there's a lot of pressure on us to solve this case. Unsurprisingly, the public are unnerved by violent murders like this one. I have no doubt it's an isolated case, but you can imagine how the locals must be feeling, knowing that the murderer's still on the loose.'

'We won't solve that problem by keeping the wrong man in custody,' Hulda pointed out coolly, but left it at that. When it came down to it, the decision was Sverrir's.

1983

Tinna

It was getting on for eleven when the phone rang. Tinna had been dozing off in front of the TV when the noisy ringing snapped her back to bleak reality. She wasn't used to receiving phone calls this late in the evening; even her parents knew better than to call her after supper. She got to her feet and hurried into the hall to answer.

'Tinna?'

She recognized Sverrir's voice immediately. What on earth could he want? Was he finally going to get around to asking her out, despite the investigation not being over yet? And the fact that she must still be a suspect . . .

'Yes, hi . . . hello . . .' She wasn't used to being flustered like this.

'This is Sverrir, from the police.'

'Yes, I know.'

'Sorry to ring so late.'

'Don't worry, it's not a problem. I was wide awake.'

'Good, good. Listen, there's something I wanted to talk to you about.'

She felt her heart beat a little faster in anticipation.

'It's about Broddi,' he said, completely wrong-footing her. 'You told me you'd seen a bloodstain on his trousers.'

She felt an overpowering sense of guilt. Damn it, she shouldn't have told that lie.

'Er, yes, that's right, I think so,' she replied. 'I think what I saw was blood.'

'Are you sure?'

She dithered, then said: 'Well, I can't be entirely sure, but that's what I thought at the time.'

'Unfortunately, we haven't been able to find any evidence that supports your claim. But we've still got Broddi in custody.'

'Oh, I see. It's always possible that I was mistaken.'

There was silence at the other end.

'Between you and me, Tinna, I need to make a decision about what to do next, whether to hold him longer or call it a day for now. I was hoping you might be able to shed some light on things for us.'

'No, or . . . no, not really. I do hope I haven't made things awkward for you.'

'Don't worry. We all make mistakes. But, in that case, I think I'll just let him go this evening.'

'Does that mean you're back to square one?'

'What? Oh no, far from it, though I can't reveal any details at this stage,' he said, quite convincingly, though there was a slightly strained note in his voice that gave her the impression that he was putting an optimistic spin on things.

There was another pause.

'Anyway, sorry to bother you, Tinna. Do remember to get in touch if there's anything – if anything occurs to you.'

Broddi was already at work when Tinna arrived at the hospital the following morning. She got there at her usual time, but he was in earlier than normal. Grateful for his newly obtained freedom, no doubt. She couldn't immediately work out why the door was unlocked, and for a moment she had a horrible sense of déjà vu, but then he called from the cafeteria.

'Is that you, Tinna?'

Immediately recognizing his voice, she felt a sharp pang in her stomach, not from fear but from a bad conscience. In a sense it had been her fault that the poor man had been locked up in the cells. But there was no getting away from the fact that Sverrir would almost certainly have investigated him sooner or later. Besides, he could still be the murderer, despite having been released without charge. She silently cursed the fact that the case had not been solved.

'Yes, it's me.' She hung her coat on its peg and went upstairs to join him. He was sitting at the table with a mug of coffee as if nothing had happened.

'Nice to see you back, Broddi,' she said warmly, though the sentiment wasn't entirely genuine.

'Yes . . . thanks. They made a mistake.'

'Anyone can make a mistake.'

'Yes.' He smiled meekly. 'It's good to be back.'

1983

Tinna

Tinna had passed another fitful night. She'd woken up thinking she was back in Yrsa's office with her dead body on that fateful morning, hearing the echo of rain in her dream, seeing the amputated fingers and the blood dripping off the desk on to the floor in time to the imaginary raindrops. But when she surfaced, she discovered that she could still hear the noise and realized that it was real: it was pouring outside.

Sitting up, she switched on the light. It was a quarter past five, which was the sort of time she'd been waking up every morning recently, and she was alone in her little flat, alone with her nightmares. Once again there was nothing for it but to get up, as if nothing was wrong, and put on some coffee to dispel the fog of sleep. She'd taken to going to bed earlier than usual in the evenings, knowing she was likely to wake up at the crack of dawn, and this had resulted in something of a vicious circle. It had also had the knock-on effect of preventing her from meeting up with friends in the evenings. Nevertheless, she was confident that the problem would go away once the case was closed and normality had returned to the hospital.

Tinna switched off the light, pulled up the duvet again and lay there staring at the darkness outside the window for a minute or two, listening to the rain. Imagining that she was somewhere – anywhere – else.

Half an hour later she was ready to face the day, wearing her yellow coat once more. Although it was now inescapably associated in her mind with the discovery of Yrsa's body, Tinna couldn't bring herself to throw it away. She couldn't afford the luxury of chucking out a perfectly good coat. The rain had stopped, as if the day was planning to go easy on her after all. She felt a dawning hope that it would turn out to be all right; not necessarily a good day, but all right; she couldn't ask for any more than that at the moment.

She went outside into the dark morning. She liked the darkness, feeling wrapped in its sheltering folds rather than afraid of it. Her car was nearby and she had all the time in the world. She filled her lungs with cold fresh air, relishing the sense of having the town to herself.

There was no reason to hurry; no one was expecting her at work this early, but at least she would be able to chalk up some overtime.

As she drove up the dark valley towards the sanatorium, however, she was overtaken by a creeping sense of foreboding that the day was going to turn out worse than expected. As if something really bad was going to happen. The premonition was so strong that she was tempted to turn round and go home, but she told herself not to be silly. Having parked her old blue Mazda in its usual spot, she walked the last stretch to the hospital. The cold was brutal, the darkness all-encompassing and the wind had begun to gust, raising a roar from the dark pines in the hospital garden – an ominously unfamiliar noise in this otherwise largely treeless landscape.

She steeled herself.

After all, how bad could it be?

1983

Tinna

'Are you sure you're OK, Tinna?' Sverrir asked. His voice conveyed nothing but warmth and friendly concern, she thought – on the surface, at least. No suspicion, not yet. 'Nobody should have to stumble across two bodies in short succession.'

She nodded.

'Are you quite sure? We can postpone this. We can . . . er, we can get someone to talk to you. An expert, like a counsellor or a doctor or something.' She sensed that he was genuinely anxious, perhaps – hopefully – because he was developing feelings for her.

'Fine, then we'll begin.' They were in the cafeteria in her wing of the sanatorium building. No one had made coffee that morning; Tinna was having to survive on the mug she'd drunk in the kitchen at home. She'd have given anything for a hot, strong black coffee right now, but she didn't like to ask.

'OK.'

'Describe it for me again – this time I'm asking you for a formal statement, as I explained. Tell me, in your own words, what happened this morning.'

Tinna drew a deep breath. 'It was just lying there when I arrived. It . . . well, I mean him . . . He was just lying there in front of me. I didn't notice anything until I was close to the building . . .'

'Describe the scene in a bit more detail, if you can, Tinna.'

'Well, it was dark, of course, but I made out this black shape on the lawn in front of the building. And when I got right up to it, I saw that it was Fridjón . . . He was just lying there. Not moving, of course. I guessed at once that he was dead, or, well, I assumed he must be.'

'Did you check?'

'Yes, of course I checked. It was an instinctive reaction, I suppose – but there was no pulse, and it was a pretty horrible sight, to be honest. It was clear that he'd . . .' She gulped, then continued: 'Clear that he'd fallen a long way. From the upstairs balcony, I suppose.'

Sverrir nodded. She waited for the question that didn't come, then felt compelled to elaborate: 'He must have thrown himself off the balcony. I can't think what else could have happened. A fall of several storeys like that. He can hardly have been on the roof.'

Again, Sverrir nodded without saying anything.

'It's just so dreadfully sad,' Tinna went on, 'that he should have chosen this way out instead of going to see you and confessing.'

'Yes, right; confess, you say . . .'

'Surely it's obvious that Fridjón must have killed Yrsa? It must have been his way of confessing. They'd known each other for years and years, so there must have been some history there that we weren't aware of, some tragedy . . .'

'Something that would lead him to kill a woman he worked with, then take his own life just over a week later?' Sverrir's voice was neutral and Tinna couldn't tell if he was agreeing with her or being sarcastic.

'Well, yes, exactly,' she said, then asked: 'Don't you think?'

'That's the question, Tinna. I can't figure out what it all means, though of course you could interpret his action like that.'

'Did he, er, did he leave a note?' she asked.

Sverrir hesitated. 'We haven't established that yet,' he answered after a beat, and she guessed that Fridjón hadn't left a note, and that Sverrir didn't quite know how to interpret what had happened, but that it would provide a neat solution: the murderer throws himself off a balcony, overwhelmed by guilt; justice is done and the mystery solved. No further action necessary. The awful gloom that lay over the hospital would lift and Tinna and her colleagues would no longer be under suspicion.

'Did you go inside at that point and call the police?' she heard him ask, possibly for the second time, as she had been briefly lost in her thoughts. She raised her eyes and smiled at him.

Yes, it would be best for everyone if this incident were

to close the case, she thought to herself. Two terrible deaths, the second cancelling out the first, however callous that sounded.

'Yes, I went straight inside,' she said.

'Did you notice anything on the way, or once you were inside? Was there anyone else around?' he asked, and she knew that the way she answered this question would be crucial.

She replied steadily, without hesitation: 'No, there was no one here but me. Who else would have been around that early?'

Almost immediately, she had the odd sensation that the walls were closing in on her, and the old, green-striped wallpaper in the cafeteria seemed even more garish than usual. She shivered as she waited for Sverrir's response, and this time he seemed to take longer to break the silence than before, though possibly that was her imagination.

'Right. So you were alone in the building?'

'What? Yes, I was alone.'

'Had Fridjón said anything?' Sverrir asked. 'Dropped any hints to suggest that he had killed Yrsa?'

Tinna shook her head, unable to come up with anything on the spot.

Her pulse began to race; she was feeling strange. All she wanted was to get out of that room and be safely at home, wrapped up in her warm duvet in its stripy cover. She just wanted to lie down, close her eyes and try to kid herself that the world was a benign, straightforward place.

'How did you get on with him?' The voice seemed to

be coming from a long way off, and she started, trying to get a grip on herself.

'What? How, who . . .'

'I'm sorry, Tinna, should we take a short break?'

'Oh no, it's fine. But is this going to take much longer?'

'No, we can stop in a minute. How did you two get on?'

'Me and Fridjón?'

He nodded and she paused to think.

'There's not much to tell, really. Fridjón was my boss, though I took my day-to-day orders from Yrsa. She was the one who hired me and told me my duties. He didn't really have anything to do with me, but then he didn't have much to do with anyone. I don't think he was very interested in people. I always found him a bit distant . . . a bit cold, maybe. As if he didn't care about me or . . . well, no, as if he didn't care about life in general.'

She hadn't been intending to phrase it quite this strongly, but it was too late to worry about that now.

'If we assume, Tinna, that he, er, jumped, would that come as a surprise to you?'

She wrinkled her brow and paused, more for show now than anything else, as the answer was self-evident.

'No, I don't think it would. He always seemed quite depressed.'

Sverrir nodded. 'Fridjón wasn't married, was he?' he asked.

'No, he wasn't married and didn't have any children. He was alone in the world, like Yrsa.'

'OK, fine, that'll do, Tinna. I'll talk to you again another time, but for now you should go home and rest.'

'Yes, I think that would be a good idea.'

She stood up, bestowing another smile on him.

She still had her coat on. For a moment she felt as if she had never left home that morning but was still in her flat by the front door, and that everything that had happened subsequently was a dream. As she left the sanatorium, stepping outside into the grey morning, she reflected on how easy it had been to lie. Disturbingly easy. Because, the truth was that she had omitted to mention the noise she'd heard when she went inside to ring the police. Somebody had sneaked out of the building, though she hadn't seen who it was. She could have sworn she'd heard an engine start up as well. She hadn't noticed any cars parked by the hospital when she arrived, apart from Fridjón's, of course, but there were plenty of places in the hospital grounds where it was possible to park unobserved. If someone had come here expressly to commit murder, the person in question would presumably have parked out of sight.

She had no intention of mentioning this to the police, though, because Fridjón's death had provided a convenient solution to the case and the next item on her agenda was to engineer a meeting with Sverrir in different, more congenial circumstances.

2012

Helgi

Elísabet had agreed to meet Helgi at a city-centre café that was fairly quiet in the middle of the day. Helgi wasn't sure if he'd recognize the woman, though he'd seen an old photograph of her in the police files: dark hair worn in a ponytail, glasses, a faraway look in her eyes, her face a little drawn, as though life had been unkind to her. Unless the picture had simply been taken on a bad day. Then he spotted her at a table in the corner, thirty years older but otherwise barely changed from the woman in the photo.

He hovered briefly, watching her and waiting to make eye contact. When she looked up, he smiled and walked over.

'Hello. Elísabet? I'm Helgi.'

'Oh, yes, Elísabet,' she confirmed hesitantly. There was a half-empty coffee cup on the table in front of her.

'Can I get you another?' he asked.

She shook her head. 'No, thanks. I don't have much time, actually.'

It was clear from the slightly hunted look in her eyes that she was lying.

Helgi took a seat.

He had explained on the phone that he was writing a dissertation about the police investigation. This was a change of tactics; previously he had said that he was writing about the deaths at the sanatorium, but he suspected he might get a better response if the focus appeared to be on the police rather than on the hospital staff. Besides, it was true; he was reviewing both aspects.

The first thing Elísabet said was: 'I know nothing about the investigation, and, anyway, it was thirty years ago; it's hard to remember details about something that happened that far in the past.' Her manner was grave, as though she was reluctant to speak about it. 'I must admit I almost said no to meeting you, but I felt I ought to be polite.'

'Thank you. I'll try not to take up too much of your time.'

'That's all right,' she said, her manner softening a little.

'So, you moved to Reykjavík?' he began, in an attempt to break the ice, though the answer was glaringly obvious, since he'd found her in the phone book. She lived in a modern block on Sóltún.

Oddly enough, the question seemed to throw her slightly.

'Yes,' she said after a moment. There was another long pause, but the quality of the silence suggested that she had more to say. 'Yes, I actually did it,' she went on. 'Last year. I swapped my house up north for a small flat down here. There was a little money left over, which I'm going to use to travel.'

She'd touched on an issue that was a constant bone of contention in Helgi's relationship; whether now was the right time to stop renting and buy a flat. He drew a deep breath, trying not to think about it, inadvertently giving Elísabet the space to continue: 'My husband died last year, so it was now or never.'

'My condolences,' Helgi said, but she didn't appear to notice. Her story seemed permeated by some deeper, longer-lasting dissatisfaction than could be explained by the loss of her husband, which she had mentioned almost as a casual aside.

'Actually, it was quite a simple decision,' she said. 'I needed a change of scene; Akureyri was haunted by too many memories of my husband and our marriage.'

'Yes, I can imagine,' Helgi replied gently. 'Are you working here in Reykjavík?'

'No, I was able to take retirement. Though now I think that was a mistake. Really, people should keep working as long as they can. Having the company of colleagues is such a lifeline.'

Helgi didn't know quite how to respond to this. 'Yes, sure, I know what you mean,' he agreed after a moment.

Elísabet seemed to radiate discontent.

'Sorry, that was beside the point,' she said abruptly. 'Anyway, tell me about your dissertation. Are you looking at the way the police handled the case, then?'

'In a manner of speaking.'

'Because there were question marks over the investigation?'

'Oh, no, nothing like that. It's more a matter of analysing the case through the lens of criminology, using the methodology we've been working with in my studies, if you see what I mean?'

'Aha.' She nodded, almost as if she were genuinely trying to take an interest in what he was saying. Perhaps she was just grateful for the chance to talk about something other than the loneliness that seemed to weigh so heavily on her.

'Do you remember the case well?'

'Well? How could I not? It sent shockwaves through the community, not just among us at the sanatorium but in the town as a whole. I never felt happy there again.'

'Did you leave your job, then? Did you move to a new workplace?'

'No, I decided to try and stick it out. They were forever restructuring things at the hospital. They were always trying to make as much use of the building as possible, so my job was quite varied, but, God, was I happy the day I walked its corridors for the last time.' She sighed. 'The place always had a bad atmosphere. There had been too many tragic deaths there back in the days when it was a sanatorium – that would have been enough of a reason on its own to make the buildings depressing, but then to have those awful things happen there. I didn't see Yrsa's body myself, but of course I heard descriptions. Tinna couldn't shut up about it.'

There was a sting in her last comment.

'What was she like to work with?'

'Tinna, you mean? She was all right. Ambitious, hard-working, always got in first in the mornings, but she'd never intended the job at the sanatorium to be permanent. We were never good enough for her; she wanted to move to a bigger hospital and she wasn't shy about telling people. Soon after the case was closed, she was out of there, and . . . and . . .' She allowed the sentence to trail off. 'The less said about that, the better, probably.'

Helgi wondered what it was she had been about to say, but didn't feel he was in any position to press her for answers.

'Were you surprised?' he asked instead.

'Surprised?'

'That Fridjón should have murdered Yrsa? Was it unexpected?'

Elísabet's face grew pensive.

'I never stopped to think about it, not really. It just happened. Something must have been going on between them that we weren't aware of. It was all very sad, but there was no point dwelling on it.'

Helgi was a little taken aback by this reply. Elísabet didn't appear to entertain the slightest doubt about Fridjón's guilt; in fact, she seemed to take the whole business in her stride.

After a pause, she added: 'Of course, I'd never have believed it beforehand, but after Yrsa was murdered, it was fairly obvious that one of us must have been involved. It was . . . well . . .' She paused again to choose her words. 'It was personal, if you know what I mean. The murderer obviously knew her. I was relieved when Fridjón ended it all, because he let the rest of us off the hook.'

'Can you imagine what could have led him to commit such a horrific crime?'

'No, I can't. But then that wasn't my job. I assume the police must have built up some kind of picture?'

Apparently not, Helgi thought to himself, but all he said aloud was: 'What did you think of the police investigation?'

'I don't really have an opinion. They did a reasonable job, as far as I know. The man in charge seemed very energetic. He was quite young, no older than I was then. I don't think he made any mistakes. And he was polite whenever he talked to me.'

'He arrested Broddi.'

'I never liked Broddi anyway. Frankly, it was a relief when they locked him up.'

'Wasn't it a mistake to arrest him, though, given what happened afterwards?'

'Well, I couldn't say. I suppose people have to find a path to the truth however they can. And it's not like he spent years in prison; it only took them a few days to correct the mistake. I doubt it changed much for him. He was rather a creepy man, to be honest; his presence made me uncomfortable. Sometimes . . .' She seemed unsure how to phrase what she wanted to say.

Helgi felt an urge to do it for her: *sometimes people can be judged by their appearance.* Isn't that what she wanted to say?

He was beginning to actively dislike this woman.

'Did you have a good working relationship with Thorri

after he took over as director?' he asked, changing the subject.

This time the silence was palpable, fraught with some uncomfortable emotion.

'We didn't work well together,' she said eventually.

'Was there any particular reason for that?' Helgi asked. He realized he was straying on to rather dubious ground here, but Elísabet didn't seem to mind his prying.

She hesitated before answering: 'The problem was, Thorri just wasn't a good manager. Things improved when he moved over to Akureyri Central. I believe he did all right there, in a more conventional role. It was the same story with him as with Tinna – the sanatorium just wasn't good enough for them.' She snorted.

It occurred to Helgi that Elísabet was the only member of staff who had stayed on at the old sanatorium to the bitter end. Tinna had moved to Reykjavík, where she still worked as a nurse. Thorri had transferred to the County Hospital, now Akureyri Central, and apparently also ran a small private clinic in the capital. And Broddi had settled in Reykjavík during his retirement. Perhaps the sanatorium had been an unhappy workplace – that could be the explanation, but Helgi thought the reason was more likely to have its roots in the two shocking deaths. Even the best workplace would find it hard to survive horrific events like that with staff morale intact.

He wondered why Elísabet had never moved to a different hospital. Had she carried on working there out of habit or just never been offered anything better? Or was it possible that something else had held her there?

'Do you have any contact with your old colleagues?'

'My old colleagues?' Elísabet repeated, as if buying time, since there could hardly be any doubt about who he meant.

'With the people who were working with you at the time of the deaths: Tinna, Broddi, Thorri . . .'

'Why on earth would you think that?' she snapped. 'I didn't like those people and didn't get on with them. I may have bumped into them now and then – Broddi and Thorri lived in Akureyri for many years, of course, and Tinna and I worked in the same profession, but I have no interest in hearing what they're up to, and I'm sure they feel the same about me.'

'Right, well, I don't want to keep you here all day,' Helgi said. He didn't have any further questions for Elísabet at present, and he wasn't enjoying her company. 'You've finished your coffee and I imagine you've got lots to do?' He tried to conceal the irony in his comment.

Elísabet rose to her feet. 'Yes, time flies, doesn't it? I need to get going, but it was good to talk to you, Helgi. Good to recall old times.' Her words rang hollow. 'You're welcome to call me again if there's anything you need to know.'

1951

Ásta

The sun had come out in Eyjafjördur at long last. It made such a difference, Ásta thought. Otherwise, the days at the sanatorium passed in drab monotony, and gloomy weather only made it harder to bear when death rampaged through the wards. The bleak, treeless moors of Vadlaheidi were now bathed in bright spring sunshine. Ásta had always felt happier in a warm climate and would have given a lot to be able to spend her retirement anywhere other than in the north of Iceland, but her finances wouldn't allow it. She and her husband didn't have a lot of money between them and their pensions would be nothing to write home about either. Trips abroad were a luxury she could only dream about, a dream she knew would never come true. Nothing would happen now to change the couple's destiny; their future was inescapably shackled to the reality of life in Iceland.

The most she could allow herself to look forward to

was the odd trip south to Reykjavík with her husband, though those were few and far between. But, to be fair, when he did get round to organizing one, the dear man pulled all the stops out. Their visit to the capital the previous year had been particularly memorable since her husband had managed to secure them tickets to a concert by the newly established Symphony Orchestra. A truly unforgettable evening.

But now the sun was out and she was feeling cheerful. She stood outside, by the wall of the hospital, sheltered from the wind, watching the children. The new boy had been allowed out at last to play with the other children, thanks entirely to her. Such a thing would never have occurred to Fridjón, who was always distracted, preoccupied with important matters, and Yrsa – well, Yrsa knew nothing about children, that was obvious. So it was up to Ásta to make sure the poor little kids got to experience a few happy hours at least. She seized the opportunity when Fridjón and Yrsa were out of the way. As it was a Sunday, there were fewer staff on duty than during the week. It gave her so much pleasure to see the smiles on the faces of the sick children, and for a moment she felt as if her own little boy were running around out there in the sunshine with the others. She even called his name, called out a couple of times without getting an answer, before she came to her senses and realized she was calling to a boy who had grown up long ago. To her embarrassment, she saw that the children were gaping at her in wonder, and she hastily looked away.

2012

Helgi

Helgi was in bed when his phone started ringing. Bergthóra was asleep and didn't appear to stir. Helgi put down his Ellery Queen book, a little annoyed at being wrenched out of the story like this.

He didn't recognize the number and hesitated briefly before deciding to answer, although it was getting on for 11 p.m. He climbed out of bed and tiptoed into the hall so as not to disturb Bergthóra. The latest wounds were beginning to heal, things were getting back to normal, but sooner or later the cycle would begin again. Still, he might as well enjoy the peace while it lasted.

'Hello,' he answered warily, unsure what to expect.

'Is that Helgi? Helgi Reykdal?'

'Yes, it is.'

'Oh, hello, this is Broddi, we spoke the day before yesterday.'

'Yes, hello, nice to hear from you,' Helgi said, rather surprised.

'Sorry to ring so late. I just wanted to apologize.'

Helgi waited without speaking.

'To apologize, you know, for how I behaved. I just wasn't in the mood to talk about what happened back then, about the arrest and all that. I know I more or less showed you the door, but I didn't mean it.'

'Don't worry about it. It's not like I have the right to demand that you tell me anything.'

'Well, fair enough, but I felt bad about it. I was wondering if I could maybe tell you my side of the story, if you had a few minutes to spare. I think it would help to talk to someone.'

'Sure, of course.' Helgi had gone into the sitting room, where he grabbed a pen and paper before settling down on the sofa to listen.

'The thing is, my life has never been easy. It's like there's been this conspiracy to keep putting obstacles in my way, over and over again.'

'A conspiracy?' Helgi found this an odd choice of word.

'Well, all I mean is that fate always seems to step in and ruin everything for me.' After a moment, Broddi added: 'Like I say, it's been difficult.'

'I see.' Helgi wasn't sure he wanted to have to listen to the story he sensed was coming.

'You see, my mother never had any money,' Broddi ploughed on, after a brief pause. 'She always struggled to make ends meet. She drank a bit too – not that much, but enough for the booze to make everything more difficult for her, if you know what I mean. She could never hold down a job for long and my childhood suffered as a result. I never met my father, and my brother didn't meet his either. Mind you, at least he knew his dad's identity: I never found out who mine was; I don't think even my mother knew for sure. Then my little brother died and it was just me and Mum. Sometimes we barely had enough to eat, though I did earn a bit at the sanatorium. And things seemed to be going in the right direction, or at least I was getting on well at work, you know. Then Mum died, leaving the flat to me, and I thought I'd find myself a good woman. I didn't want to be alone, you know how it is.' He fell silent and Helgi could hear his heavy breathing over the phone. 'I'd even started seeing a woman. But then I was arrested. That policeman, Sverrir, he arrested me, I remember it like it was yesterday. There was some woman with him, she didn't say much, but they made out I'd killed Yrsa, and soon everyone – I mean *everyone* – believed I'd killed her. It didn't make any difference that I was released in the end, because you can never shake off a stigma like that in a small community. Everybody knew everyone else in Akureyri, and people were on their guard against me afterwards. Imagine going through that, Helgi.'

'I can believe it was tough.'

'I don't think you can put yourself in my shoes, I'm afraid, but I'll tell you what it was like. I'll describe it for you as well as I can, Helgi. You know how some days come along – beautiful summer days, when you wake up with the sun streaming through the window and think to yourself, *This is going to be a wonderful day*. You dare to let yourself look forward to it – it's all right to do that once in a while. Can you picture it, Helgi? You lie there in bed, looking out of the window at the sunny morning, and you dare – *dare* – to look forward to the rest of the day. Then you close your eyes, Helgi, and when you open them again you're outside the house and the sun has gone in. It's evening now and it's started to rain, and the drops land on your face, land on your cheeks and turn into tears, because you're crying, Helgi, you're crying because you just don't understand what happened. All you know is that you missed out on that one beautiful day and now you're standing outside in the rain, cold and alone. And then . . .' He paused for breath, before picking up the thread again: 'And then, Helgi, you realize that someone stole that summer's day from you, someone stole your life, maybe without realizing, maybe deliberately. There you have my life in a nutshell. It just disappeared – my best years gone. The fact is, I was driven out of my home town and forced to move to Reykjavík.'

He fell silent, perhaps only to draw breath, but Helgi seized this chance to jump in.

'I really don't know what to say, Broddi. Do you mean that your arrest was to blame for all of this?'

'Well, it might sound like a big claim,' Broddi answered, more calmly now, 'but I'm not in any doubt. It's hard to put yourself in the shoes of an innocent man who has been arrested and accused of a terrible crime – an absolutely terrible crime, Helgi. Even you, as a criminologist, can hardly imagine what it's like.'

'You may be right. But I do at least know how important it is for justice to be done, however late in the day.'

There was a silence on the line.

'Are you suggesting that they're going to reopen the case?' Broddi asked at last.

'That's not up to me,' Helgi replied, not entirely honestly. After all, he would be joining the police sooner or later, there wasn't much doubt of that, and, besides, the way this case was shaping up almost made him want to ditch his dissertation and launch himself into a formal investigation, in an effort to get to the bottom of what really did happen in 1983.

'I suppose it's too late now, anyway?' Broddi said, and there was no mistaking the sadness in his voice. 'Far too late.'

'Look, thanks for calling, Broddi. Thanks for telling me your story.'

'Keep it to yourself, will you? I didn't mean to come out with all that stuff, but sometimes your feelings run away with you, especially at my age.'

'I'll let you know if I get anywhere with my enquiries,' Helgi said. 'And maybe we can have another coffee some time, if we get a chance. I'll be completely taken up with my dissertation for the next few weeks, though.'

'Call me any time. I'd really like to help.'

They rang off, and Helgi made a mental note to have another go at talking to Tinna as soon as possible. He wanted to get a sense of the bigger picture, and intuition told him that he wouldn't be able to do that without her.

2012

Helgi

This time the damage was more serious than usual.

Their television, their new flatscreen, lay smashed to pieces on the floor. Helgi knew this had to stop. A new TV would cost an arm and a leg, and there was no guarantee that they'd be able to afford another flatscreen any time soon, but that wasn't the main issue. Things just couldn't go on like this – all these endless arguments and fights. They'd made a hell of a racket too. Helgi was only surprised their neighbour hadn't called the police again. He was grateful for small mercies at least.

He swept the pieces of a broken vase into a dustpan but decided to leave the television where it was for now. It could wait until morning, since the damage had already been done. He didn't particularly enjoy watching TV anyway, and he could keep up with the news on his computer. If anything, it would simply mean he had more time to read than before. The Ellery Queen book had been returned to the shelf. It hadn't aged well and he had given up around the halfway mark. He pulled down another book instead that he knew he would enjoy, one of the first Icelandic translations of an Agatha Christie novel. *The Murder of Roger Ackroyd*, it was called, one of his absolute favourites. The translation had stood the test of time quite well, although it was from 1941, the language transporting Helgi back to a vanished world. This was exactly the kind of relaxation he needed right now. Bergthóra had fled into the bedroom as usual and locked herself in. Fine. He was used to sleeping on the sofa.

There was a knock on the door.

It gave him such a start that he dropped the old volume on the floor and swore aloud.

Could it be the police again?

What was he supposed to say this time to get rid of them?

There was another bout of knocking.

He hurried into the hall and checked his appearance in the mirror. Oh hell, his shirt was torn, but at least there was no blood this time.

He took down a jacket from a peg in the entrance hall and put it on. It might look a bit odd, but it would be worse to be caught with his shirt in tatters.

When he opened the door, he saw to his surprise that their neighbour was standing outside, dressed, as usual, as if he'd just woken up after a night on the tiles, his hair a mess, his shirt only half buttoned. Short of breath due to his excess kilos.

'Helgi,' he said, looking irate. He stood very still, as if

marking his territory, like he owned the house, which was far from the truth.

'Hello, I was just on my way out.' Helgi smiled at him, though he had never felt less like smiling at anyone.

'You've been making an unacceptable amount of noise again. You know I've got small kids.' The neighbour raised his voice, his words emerging in a splutter. Getting worked up didn't suit him.

'Look, we had an accident – a vase got broken. The ceiling must be paper thin, judging by the way you keep complaining.'

'Well, it just won't do. It frightens the kids.'

'I suppose I should be grateful you didn't call the police this time.'

'Well, I . . . I . . .'

'I know you set the cops on me.' Narrowing his eyes, Helgi added, stretching the truth a little: 'You know I'm in the police myself, don't you?'

'What? No, I wasn't aware of that.'

'Well, you are now. And let me tell you, I'm not happy about the police's precious time being wasted on this kind of nonsense.'

'Could I maybe talk to your wife?' the neighbour asked, after an awkward pause.

'Why do you want to talk to her? She's got nothing to say to you, though she's got more patience with you than I have. As far as I'm concerned, I've had it up to here with you sticking your nose into our affairs.'

The neighbour snorted. 'I just can't put up with this any longer – I mean, it's happening almost on a daily basis.'

'Then maybe you should move,' Helgi said, and slammed the door in his face.

He took off his jacket, hurried back into the sitting room and settled down again on the sofa with the Agatha Christie, his hands shaking.

He realized he'd forgotten the music. There was nothing better than reading to a soothing jazz soundtrack, but he was comfortable now and didn't want to move.

Even the empty wine bottle on the table, directly in his eyeline, could stay where it was for the moment, though it was a reminder of their quarrels, of all the fights; not just a reminder but also, in a way, the cause. Though the roots lay deeper.

The cover of the book was plain, no picture on the front, no blurb on the back, nothing to distract attention from the contents, just the title and the author's name. He'd read it so often before, but the moment he saw the first line on the first page, he was transported into the world of the story, where nothing bad could happen to him.

1983

Tinna

That evening, Tinna found she couldn't stop shivering. She had tried getting into bed, but it didn't help; the uncontrollable tremors continued. And that wasn't all; she had been feeling a little spooked by the darkness in her bedroom, afraid to close her eyes, watching every shadow. At length, she had given up, got out of bed again, turned on the lights and decided to have a hot bath. It was a luxury she indulged in far too rarely and probably exactly what she needed now after such a difficult day. More than difficult – surreal. Tinna knew that if she closed her eyes again, the nightmares would be twofold. As if it wasn't bad enough being haunted by ghastly images of Yrsa's dead body, she would now have to contend with Fridjón's too.

The scalding bath temporarily helped to disperse her thoughts. She lit a candle but didn't quite have the courage to switch off the light in the bathroom. As she lay back and relaxed, the hot water enveloped her body and banished her shivers. She allowed her eyes to close and her head to sink slowly under the surface, then concentrated on holding her breath for as long as she could, feeling all her other worries receding.

Even in her cosy flat she was susceptible to feeling nervous sometimes, unaccustomed as she was to living alone. At those times she could feel herself regressing back into the little girl who used to be too scared to walk around her parents' house alone at night. It didn't take much to trigger this state: a noise she couldn't identify, a feeling of unease. The fact the flat was on the ground floor didn't help, since there was always the possibility that a burglar might try to break in. That was her worst nightmare – waking up to find a figure looming over her bed. Of course, nothing like that had ever happened, but the recent events at the hospital had given rise to all kinds of irrational fears, and now all she wanted was to flee to her parents' house and sleep there. But that was out of the question; she was determined to behave like an adult, despite everything that had happened.

No one's going to hurt me, she told herself as her head broke the surface. She repeated this mantra again and again, until she'd started to say the words aloud, whispering them so quietly that only the walls could hear.

But memories of this morning, of the last few days, crowded in on her again in the silence. It seemed there was no way of escaping them.

The tiles on the bathroom walls were dark red and patterned with roses, not at all to Tinna's taste. She'd wanted to tear them out the day she moved in, but she still hadn't got round to it and knew that getting rid of them wouldn't be cheap. There was also the subconscious awareness that she wouldn't be living here for long. It was her first flat, little more than a stopgap. The plan was, sooner or later, to move south to Reykjavík.

The dark red shade and lurid flowers grated on Tinna so badly that they almost made her feel ill. They gave her such a stifling sense of being stuck in the past. She lay there perfectly still, staring up at the ceiling. At least that was a neutral white. It was better to feel nothing at all, she reflected, than to feel stressed.

It was then that she heard the noise. A furtive rustling, like someone moving around in the back garden. The bathroom window, which was covered with grey, frosted-glass film, faced directly on to the garden. No one ever went round there – no one had any reason to be there, least of all in this cold weather, in the dark. She must have misheard.

She sat up in the bath and held herself absolutely still, as still as she could, the water rippling faintly, and now she could hear nothing but her own breathing reverberating off the tasteless tiles. The roses seemed to be closing in on her. Her breathing kept coming faster, her fear intensifying, but she tried to convince herself that the sound had been purely imaginary, and there was nothing to be frightened of. It was probably a cat, or something else equally harmless, but the events at the hospital had left her so strung out that suddenly even perfectly ordinary noises seemed menacing. She sat there, rigid, straining her ears.

All was quiet outside. She mustn't let herself become paranoid; things were bad enough already.

She closed her eyes, letting her tense muscles relax, and prepared to submerge her head once more and empty her mind.

Then she heard it again. This time there was no doubt; there was somebody outside, disturbingly close to the window, almost as if the unknown person wanted her to know they were there. The window was open a crack to allow the steamy air to escape and the bathroom light was on, so it must be obvious that she was in there.

She sat up again in a swirl of water, all her muscles tensing with fear. It was bad enough being alone in the flat in normal circumstances, but now there was definitely somebody out there.

Had she locked the front door?

She began to tremble.

Her back was to the bathroom window and she couldn't summon up the courage to look round, though she knew this was only putting off the inevitable. If somebody meant to do her harm, as far-fetched as that might sound, she would be a sitting duck. The first thing she had to do was get out of the bath and on to her feet. Taking a deep breath, she stood up quickly, unable to avoid a loud sloshing sound, and focused hard on keeping her balance in the slippery tub.

Then she gave in to the temptation to snatch a glance over her shoulder, against her better judgement, curiosity getting the better of common sense.

There was a faint shadow falling across the window, a figure standing outside in the dark, apparently trying to peer in through the filmed glass.

She felt so exposed and vulnerable, caught stark naked like this in the illuminated bathroom, alone in the flat. The terror was overwhelming, like nothing she had ever experienced before.

Recoiling violently, she lost her footing and toppled over backwards. The fall felt simultaneously unreal and terrifying, the moment seeming to stretch out for an eternity, and she was convinced it would be her last – that she would hit her head and drown. But somehow she managed to break the fall with her arms, landing in the water with a great splash but without injuring herself. She clambered out of the tub in a panic, the shadow on the window still there, barely moving, but there was no question that it was a person.

Tinna fled into the hall, her wet feet skidding on the lino, and made straight for the front door, where she jerked at the handle. It was securely locked, thank God. Then she dived into the little spare room, the only windowless room in the flat, and locked herself in, though she suspected the door would provide little protection if put to the test. On second thoughts, she pushed the desk against it. All the time, her mind was frantically searching for explanations as to who the intruder could be and why this was happening to her. The visit had to be connected to the deaths at the hospital. What else?

Tinna shrank back into a corner in the impenetrable blackness, naked, trembling and utterly alone, listening to the crashing of her heart and struggling to get her panic under control.

1983

Tinna

The blue-checked tablecloth, the grey-blue dinner plates, the plain cutlery and Danish crystal-glass carafe of water, it was all so familiar, all so comfortingly old-fashioned and homely, just what Tinna needed this evening, the day after Fridjón's death – the day after a prowler had loomed outside her bathroom window, almost scaring the living daylights out of her.

She couldn't have cowered in the pitch-black, windowless room for more than half an hour, but it had felt like an eternity. Her eyes had slowly grown accustomed to the gloom, which was relieved only by a faint line of light showing under the door, but it had taken her a long time to still her trembling, and for a while she wasn't sure she'd have the nerve to leave her refuge at all. In the end, though, she had steeled herself and crept out into the hall, her teeth chattering from cold now as well as fear. She had paused to listen at every step, and turned out the lights on the way, before finally satisfying herself that the prowler had gone. After that she had gone round drawing all the curtains and making sure that the windows were securely fastened. Needless to say, it had taken her ages to get to sleep and, when she finally dropped off, her rest had been troubled by a series of nightmares. She couldn't remember what she'd dreamt, not in any detail, only the vague sensation of menace.

Now, after another strange day at work, she was sitting at the supper table at her parents' house in the neighbouring street, grateful for their company, though she dreaded having to discuss the goings-on at the hospital.

There was roast lamb for dinner and the delicious smell took her back to Sunday evenings in her childhood and teens – unvarying, monotonous Sundays and overcooked meat, she had thought at the time. She'd fled the tedium the first chance she'd got, going away to university in the capital, then getting her own flat when she moved back to Akureyri. And now she was planning to look for work in Reykjavík, as far away from her parents as she could get. Yet in this moment there was nowhere else she would rather be.

'Are you sure you don't want to spend the night here?' her father asked, not for the first time that evening. He was much more demonstrative and affectionate by nature than her mother, and had worried and fussed over Tinna ever since she could remember. Her mother, Gudrún, in contrast, had an icy manner and said little, though when she did speak she could be incredibly bossy and was quick to make enemies. She had been getting on Tinna's nerves for years, which had no doubt played a big part in her desire to leave home. Tinna loved her mother, of course, and her mother loved her in return, but they just didn't get on. Not that Gudrún got on with anyone, except perhaps Tinna's father. Between them there seemed to be a tacit agreement to tolerate and even love each other.

'Quite sure, Dad. I like being in my flat, and it's only round the corner.'

'Yes, I know that, but this is hardly a normal situation, Tinna. These deaths – the whole thing's enough to send shivers down one's spine. It's hardly normal, is it? And for you to discover both bodies – terrible, just terrible.'

'Oh, leave her alone,' Gudrún snapped, her tone acid, as usual. 'Tinna's a grown-up. She can take care of herself. Anyway, it's obvious, isn't it? Fridjón must have bumped off the poor woman, then thrown himself to his death.' As an afterthought, she added: 'I remember Fridjón from the old days; he never made a good impression on me. He was arrogant, and there was something untrustworthy about him too. You should be able to trust a doctor.'

Typical Gudrún, Tinna thought, passing judgement on her fellow citizens, even when they were dead. Personally, Tinna had always liked Fridjón.

There was no way she could mention last night's mysterious prowler to her parents, or the fact that she had heard somebody leaving the hospital building the morning she'd discovered Fridjón's body. She meant to keep that information to herself for now. If she notified the police, it would only make matters worse and prolong the investigation. Whereas it would suit her to have the case closed as soon as possible. Because then she could set about making a serious play for Sverrir.

'How are things at the sanatorium these days, Tinna?' her father asked. 'I don't suppose people can be getting much work done. Anyway, you're only taking care of paperwork for the County Hospital, aren't you?'

'Well, we're doing our best to keep things going, in the circumstances.'

'Yes, I can imagine,' he said. 'Have a Coke, love. It'll give you a bit of energy.' Drinking Coke with the Sunday roast lamb was another family tradition, one glass bottle per person, and they were observing the custom tonight, although it wasn't a Sunday. Tinna's bottle remained unopened and, ideally, she'd have liked something stronger, but she wasn't used to drinking alcohol in front of her parents.

Her father handed her a bottle opener and she cracked off the lid and took a swig.

'I'm not planning to stay there much longer anyway,' she announced.

'Oh?' her mother exclaimed, her brows snapping together in a frown.

'No, I'm thinking of applying for something in Reykjavík – not immediately, you know, but in a year or two.'

'Oh dear, we do so enjoy having you back here with us,' her father lamented. 'But, of course, it's your life.'

'The thing is, I don't always feel easy at the sanatorium,' Tinna said, after a short silence. And it was true.

'There's too much history there, too much . . . well, too many past tragedies, I suppose. And these recent deaths have had an effect too, you know?' She realized that it was her father she was talking to, as these weren't the kind of sentiments she would think of sharing with her mother, although Gudrún was sitting at the table with them.

'Things used to be pretty bleak in the old days,' her father agreed. 'TB was such a deadly disease, such a cruel fate. You never knew when it would strike. It used to be one of the biggest killers in Iceland, especially in Reykjavík, before they eradicated it. That seems hard to believe now. The worst part was hearing about the children who were infected. Some survived; others weren't so lucky. My friend Oddur got it and spent a long time in the sanatorium, though he made an amazingly good recovery in the end. But the building used to be associated in people's minds with death, though I'm sure that's changed – or had changed, until this happened.'

2012

Thorri

It was eccentric of the young man to want to look into that old case after all these years, Thorri thought. Personally, he had done his best not to dwell on the memories, but pushed them aside and concentrated on his job, a policy that had worked out quite well in the long run. His transfer from the old sanatorium to Akureyri County Hospital had been a relief, as by then he'd been heartily sick of the gloomy corridors and the pale ghosts that seemed to lurk in every dark corner.

Thorri eked out his income by travelling to Reykjavík every couple of weeks to perform surgery at his own private clinic, and the next trip was planned for the following Monday. He had told this young man Helgi that he would be prepared to meet him then, though in reality he was reluctant.

He thought about his old colleagues – those who were still alive. Tinna and Elísabet had both moved to

Reykjavík, whereas he had resisted the temptation, preferring to be a big fish in a smaller pond, and no one could deny that he had made a success of his career in Akureyri. For a long time, it had been his father who held him there, directly or indirectly, until the old man eventually died, at a surprisingly advanced age, given his lifestyle. Although he had been on the streets for many years, there had been periods of sobriety when he'd been taken in by Thorri and had proved a kind and loving grandfather. But then, without warning, he'd vanish again, fallen off the wagon, back on the streets. The old man had been highly intelligent in his youth and had seemed destined for a medical career, but the pressure had been too much for him and he'd ended up divorced and in the gutter.

Then there was Broddi. Thorri hadn't seen the caretaker for years, but apparently he'd moved to Reykjavík too. He'd been living under a cloud ever since his arrest, and had had a tough time of it in Akureyri as a result. People could be cruel, especially to a man like Broddi, who was a bit of a social outcast, and it didn't help that the investigation had never been satisfactorily closed; it had just lost momentum after Fridjón's suicide and been quietly dropped. That is, the police had never actually established for certain whether it had been suicide, but it was fairly obvious that the man hadn't fallen off the balcony by accident – the handrail hadn't been that low.

By agreeing to Helgi's request, Thorri felt as if he had agreed to open a door into the past, a door that he would have preferred to keep locked. As the faces of the people involved appeared before his mind's eye, he felt increasingly edgy about this meeting. But he couldn't say no. There was something about the old case that made it impossible to forget, impossible to dismiss from one's mind, though Thorri himself had emerged from the situation remarkably unscathed, in a manner of speaking. As far as he was aware, he had never even been a suspect. Perhaps he had been too young and inexperienced for it to occur to anyone that he could have held a grudge against Yrsa.

He supposed that this was where the deception lay, in a sense. Because while he'd had no axe to grind with Yrsa, the same could not be said of his relationship with Fridjón.

2012

Helgi

The car crawled along in the late-afternoon traffic; it was bumper to bumper on Hringbraut and Helgi had to make a superhuman effort not to give in to frustration. The congestion had definitely become worse since he went abroad for his studies, with ever more vehicles on the road. No doubt the increase in tourist numbers was partly to blame. The Radio 2 afternoon show was playing over his old speakers, which sounded so muffled and tinny nowadays that the programme might as well have been coming from the car sitting next to him in the traffic jam. The topic of today's discussion was the property market. Normally Helgi would have tuned out at this point, but recently Bergthóra had been putting pressure on him to buy a place, arguing that there was no point renting for ever and that they should start saving as much money as they could before the end of the year, in the hope that they'd have enough to put down a deposit on a small flat in the spring. The interviewee on today's programme was an economist who used to be a well-known musician. In Iceland, Helgi reflected, everyone needed at least two jobs in order to survive. He and Bergthóra had accumulated nothing but debts back in the days when he was temping for the police and she was working as a developmental therapist. But now he had the prospect of a respectable salary if he accepted the offer of a managerial position in Reykjavík CID.

The man on the radio was saying that property prices were predicted to rise rapidly in the next few years, so Helgi supposed it would be a wise move to act now, even though this would mean living in the suburbs and being stuck in traffic jams like this every day on his commute to and from work. The trouble was that Helgi was finding it hard to make future plans that included Bergthóra. In all honesty, he wasn't sure he wanted to buy a property with her, wasn't even sure they would stay together or when that particular bubble would burst with an almighty bang. He kept postponing the decision, again and again, thinking no further than plans for the next weekend, next month, even the summer holidays, while the bigger decisions were put on hold. Like getting on the property ladder or starting a family, in whichever order.

If only he had inherited something more substantial than his father's books, which, although infinitely precious to him, were of no monetary value at all, then perhaps he could have followed the advice of the economist on the radio and invested in a place on his own. But there was no chance of that at present.

Abandoning this train of thought, he focused his mind on the coming interview. He was on his way to see Thorri, the doctor from Akureyri, who'd explained that he spent at least two weeks out of every month in Reykjavík and had agreed to the request for a quick meeting.

Thorri answered the door of his clinic himself, his hair neatly combed back, wearing a white coat over a white shirt and a red tie. He was tall, with an intelligent face, piercing eyes and the air of a man who was used to getting his own way. Almost the diametric opposite of Broddi.

The waiting room – or reception area – looked as if it had been cut out of a lifestyle magazine. It was spotlessly clean and tidy, with modern sofas and coffee table, no dog-eared magazines; in fact, nothing to show that anyone else had ever been there. The only painting on the wall, a large abstract canvas, gave the effect of staring off into a distant horizon.

'The traffic must have been bad,' Thorri commented, glancing at the clock. Although his tone was casual, it was clear that he was referring to Helgi's late arrival. Then, without waiting for a response, he gave an on-off smile and said: 'We'd better take a seat in my office.'

His office turned out to be, if anything, even more coldly impersonal than the waiting room: chilly, clinical, all black furniture, white walls and a desk bare apart from a laptop. It was hard to imagine that anyone actually worked there.

'Thanks for taking the time to see me,' Helgi said. 'I'm sure you're extremely busy.'

Thorri took a seat behind his desk and gestured to Helgi to sit down. The only other chair was conspicuously less comfortable than the doctor's, like a tangible demonstration of the power relationship in the room.

'Yes, there's plenty to do, but then there always is in my profession.' Thorri's voice betrayed a definite hint of arrogance.

'So you work both here and in Akureyri, do you?'

'Yes, that's right. I work at the hospital there, then I have my private practice here in town – I used to share it with a couple of other doctors, but now I have it to myself, which is much more convenient.'

'You're not based at the same hospital as before, are you? The old sanatorium, I mean?'

'Good God, no!' Thorri exclaimed indignantly. 'I left the sanatorium years ago. There's still a limited operation there, but it didn't offer me a sufficiently challenging environment.'

'I see.' Helgi nodded. 'How come you originally went to work there, then?'

'What? Oh, I was doing a study on tuberculosis, reviewing old cases, medical records and so on, but I only ever intended to make use of the facilities there for a limited period. It was a research project, well funded, but—'

'But then Fridjón died and you took over his job as director?'

'I was forced by circumstance to take over, Helgi. What else was I supposed to do? The position held no appeal for me, but the director died – he threw himself off the hospital balcony. I was there for just over a year, if I remember right. I tidied things up a bit and sorted out the management side, then I got myself transferred to the County Hospital at the earliest possible opportunity.'

Helgi jotted down some notes, mainly for appearances' sake. Normally he relied on his memory, which generally stood him in good stead.

'You tidied things up, you say?'

'Yes.'

'How do you mean?'

'I reorganized the finances.' Thorri paused briefly. 'And I sacked Broddi.'

'Why?'

'He'd been in police custody, suspected of murder. Isn't that enough?'

'He was released without charge.'

'All the same, he was a bit of a weirdo,' Thorri said, then added hastily, enunciating with exaggerated care: 'Don't quote me directly in your dissertation, will you? I'm speaking off the record here, so I'm not expressing myself quite as cautiously as I would do otherwise.'

Helgi suddenly wondered if Thorri had been drinking. If so, he hid it well.

'How did he take it?'

'Broddi?'

'Yes.'

'Badly, of course, as you can imagine, but it's not my responsibility to see that everyone has a job.'

There was something about the doctor's manner – a slight lack of caution, perhaps, accompanied by that painstaking enunciation of his words – that gradually convinced Helgi he had indeed been drinking.

'How did you originally get interested in tuberculosis?' he asked.

'Interested?'

'Well, you said you'd been writing a study or research paper when you got the job.'

'I can't see what that's got to do with anything,' Thorri replied, visibly controlling his temper. 'The chance just landed in my lap. Fridjón sorted it out for me. A sound man, Fridjón.'

'I don't doubt it. Where had you been before?'

'Been before? Before the sanatorium, you mean? I was working as a doctor somewhere else.'

'Was that in the countryside too?'

'Er, yes.' The doctor seemed oddly thrown. 'Yes, in Hvammstangi. I saw the sanatorium position as a good opportunity to move to a bigger town.'

'I see. Then Fridjón went and threw himself off the balcony.'

Thorri's eyes widened slightly at this.

Helgi added: 'As you put it yourself.'

'Oh, right, yes.'

'Was that indisputable?'

'How do you mean?'

'Maybe I've misunderstood,' Helgi said innocently, 'but the impression I got was that the case had never been satisfactorily solved.'

'Not satisfactorily solved?' Thorri snorted. 'Of course

it was solved. Why should the man have acted like that if he wasn't guilty of murdering Yrsa?'

'Someone could have pushed him.'

'Are you completely mad?' Thorri shoved back his chair and got to his feet. 'I have to say that I can't figure you out at all, Helgi. I meet a lot of people every day and I reckon I'm a pretty good judge of character, but I don't understand what it is you're up to. Are you really writing a dissertation about the case or is that just a cover story?'

Helgi rose to his feet as well. He wasn't prepared to put up with this kind of rudeness, though he was aware he might have strayed off the subject a little in his questioning.

'Yes, I am genuinely writing a dissertation. I'm doing an MA in criminology, as I explained to you . . .' Helgi thought for a moment, then went on, acting on a hunch that the doctor had something to hide: 'Though, as a matter of fact, I'm going to be taking over a senior position with Reykjavík CID in a few weeks' time.'

Thorri seemed taken aback by this.

'Ah, well, I apologize for getting a bit heated,' he said, 'but I don't know what you're hoping to gain from these questions. I'm happy to assist you as far as I can, but . . . but surely you're not intending to reopen the case after all these years?'

'Far from it.'

'Shall we sit down again, then? Can I offer you a drink?'

'A soda water would be good.'

'I've got some chilled white wine in the fridge if you'd prefer.'

'No, thanks. I'm driving.'

'I'll fetch you a soda water, then,' the doctor said, and went out, returning almost immediately with a small bottle in one hand and a glass of white wine in the other.

He handed Helgi the soda water and took his seat behind the desk again. 'Long day,' he said, a little defensively.

'I know what you mean,' Helgi replied. 'Tell me: the investigation at the time – what was your impression of it? Did it seem thorough?'

'I have to admit that I don't remember much about it. The officer in charge was quite young.'

'His name was Sverrir,' Helgi supplied.

'It's possible, I don't remember,' Thorri said, and took a sip of wine. 'He was pretty thorough, from what I recall. Naturally, he talked to me, and I tried to provide him with what help I could. Not that I ever got the sense that I myself was under suspicion, you understand.' Thorri made it sound like a preposterous idea.

'What was the atmosphere like at the sanatorium while this was going on? It must have been quite stressful for all concerned?'

'Yes, I expect so . . . Fortunately, the situation didn't last long, though. I mean, I never had the feeling I was in any danger myself, in spite of what happened to Yrsa. Perhaps I'd suspected old Fridjón all along – subconsciously, that is. Sensed that there was some unfinished business between them that had nothing to do with me . . .' Thorri took another mouthful of wine. 'Had nothing to do with the rest of us, I mean.'

1983

Tinna

Before leaving her parents' house, Tinna had to turn down yet another offer from her father to stay the night. It went without saying that she was grateful for his concern; it was kindly meant, and maybe not such a crazy idea after all. Perhaps it would have done her good to have a change of surroundings, even if only for one night; to retreat into childhood, to when life had been less complicated. Sleeping in her old bed, she might have had pleasant dreams instead of reliving the events at the hospital on a loop. All the same, she had declined the offer, and that was that, so now she was headed home. It wasn't far, and she set off slowly, telling herself there was nothing to be afraid of. The town was shrouded in darkness and she allowed the night to seep inside her, gradually filling her mind and body, until suddenly she heard a noise that seemed out of place and she flinched, all her courage evaporating in an instant. She was so alarmed that she broke into a run, sprinting as fast as she could, heart beating fit to burst, groping in vain for her keys as she went. Could she have left them at her parents' house? She didn't dare glance over her shoulder, but then her fingers closed over the keys in her pocket. She opened the front door with a loud rattle, shot inside and slammed it shut behind her. In normal circumstances she might not even have bothered to lock it when she went out, but this time she had taken great care to ensure that she locked it behind her when she left and she was very careful to secure it again now that she was inside.

She switched on the light in the hall, went into the bedroom, switched on the lamp there as well and sat down on the bed, trying to catch her breath. The noise she'd heard had probably been a cat on the prowl or something equally innocent, but God she'd been frightened. Things couldn't go on like this. She had to convince herself that last night's experience had been an isolated incident that had nothing to do with her. That had to be it; had to be.

Tinna usually relaxed by watching television in the evenings, though the stuff on offer tended to be fairly uninspiring. Dropping off in front of the box was the best way to get to sleep, if she could do so before the schedule ended. The burbling voices made her feel she wasn't entirely alone. But although she would gladly have had the TV for company tonight, sadly that wasn't an option, as there was no broadcast on Thursdays. Instead, she decided to see if she could distract herself by reading. She closed and locked her bedroom door and drew the curtains, making sure there weren't any gaps, then lay down on top of the bedclothes with a copy of *The Week*, not quite ready to go to bed yet as it still wasn't that late.

The ringing of the phone filtered into her dreams and woke her. She hadn't got very far into *The Week* before she flaked out. She sat up with a jerk, then got warily off the bed. The last time someone had rung her this late at night it had been Sverrir, but he was unlikely to be calling now, since the case was as good as closed, though he and Hulda were apparently still in town, tying up loose ends.

She hesitated for a moment before picking up the receiver, instinct warning her not to answer, but in the end she felt compelled to. The need to know who was calling was just too strong.

'Hello?' she said, unable to keep the tremor out of her voice.

There was someone at the other end, she could tell, but the person didn't speak.

'Hello? Who is it?'

The silence continued, but there was no question that there was somebody there, listening to her but deliberately not answering. She considered hanging up, but stopped herself, anxious to find out what the caller wanted. Then she threw a hasty glance around, as if afraid the person on the line was watching her, though of course that was impossible. Tinna was becoming increasingly unnerved. This couldn't be a coincidence, could it?

The menacing silence continued. 'Who is this? My name's Tinna. Have you got the wrong number?' She tried to sound confident, even annoyed, but the tremor in her voice gave her away.

There was a rustle on the line, then a click as the caller hung up. She felt as if the phone call had lasted for ages, though it had probably only been a few seconds, the silence having the effect of stretching out time.

She put down the receiver, stared at the dark grey telephone for a moment, then took a step backwards, as if it were threatening her.

No one had done anything to her, not yet, but the threat was real. Someone wanted her to know they were there. And the only person she could think of was the man or woman who had sneaked out of the sanatorium yesterday morning when she discovered Fridjón's body. She'd heard someone but had withheld the information from the police. Perhaps whoever it was had spotted her and wanted to ensure that she kept her mouth shut.

On the other hand, she could be reading too much into the whole thing. An unknown person prowling around in the garden yesterday evening, a wrong number now . . . She sincerely hoped so.

But she needed to find out who had called. She took a deep breath.

Her first thought was to ring Sverrir, though it was so late he would probably have left work by now.

She phoned the police station on the off chance, introduced herself and asked to speak to him.

'Tinna?' The surprise in his voice was obvious.

'Yes, hello, is this a bad moment?'

'Er, no, not at all. It's lucky you caught me, as I was about to go home. Back to the guest house, I mean.'

He sounded far more upbeat than he had the last time they talked.

'Oh, right, it wasn't important really. I just wanted to see if you could help me with something.'

'Of course.'

'The thing is, I got a phone call just now, and I kind of need to know who it was.'

'Oh? What do you mean? Was it something serious?'

'No, not at all. And it has nothing to do with the case or anything. It was just a bit unsettling. It's happened before, several times,' she lied. 'Long before this business with Yrsa and Fridjón.'

'Ah, I see . . .' He hesitated. 'Has someone been harassing you?'

'What? Oh no,' she said. 'I don't suppose it would be possible to find out anyway . . .'

'Sure it would. I just need to order a trace.'

'A trace?'

'Yes, by the phone company. It shouldn't take long. Is everything OK apart from that?' he asked, sounding as if he genuinely cared.

'Yes, of course, everything's fine,' she replied, trying to prevent her fear and anxiety from breaking through. 'Well, thanks so much for the help. I'll explain things properly later. It's just that I occasionally get these odd phone calls.'

'I'm sorry to hear that. And it's no problem to help,' he

said, but Tinna got the feeling he was going out of his way to assist her and that it wasn't really as straightforward as he was pretending. 'I'll give you a call, hopefully tomorrow or the next day, then,' he said, 'and let you know what I've found out.'

1983

Tinna

Tinna had overcome her reluctance and made herself go in to work. Broddi was there, a chastened figure these days, skulking along the walls like a broken man, and she felt sorry for him, even guilty, aware that she was partly to blame for his arrest and detention.

Thorri, in contrast, seemed to be thriving. He had been asked to step in as acting director and had undergone a transformation in the forty-eight hours since Fridjón's death. He had immediately started to demonstrate character traits that Tinna didn't particularly appreciate, though previously she had liked him fine. These included a patronizing manner of talking down to people, ignoring their suggestions and making it clear that he meant to run everything himself rather than delegating tasks and moulding his staff into a team. It seemed that not everyone was suited to a managerial role. This only strengthened Tinna's resolve to move to a new workplace the first chance she got.

Then there was Elísabet. Tinna was working directly under her now, which was unquestionably an improvement; one small ray of light in the prevailing darkness. Yet although Elísabet was polite and friendly on the surface – Tinna had no complaints there – there was something slightly off about her manner.

The day crawled by, an uneasy silence hanging over the sanatorium.

Perhaps the effect was temporary, a reaction to the recent tragedy that had played out there, or perhaps the change was permanent and the place would never be the same again. By the time Tinna left the building at the end of the day, emerging into the cold to begin her weekend, she had more or less made up her mind to take the following week off, if possible, and drive south to Reykjavík to test the waters in the job market there. See if she could get a position at a hospital or a nursing home. Enjoy a complete change of scene.

But for now she planned to have a relaxing evening, going out for a meal with Bibba and some other friends at Bautinn, Akureyri's most popular restaurant. The nightlife up here might be a bit limited, she thought, but Reykjavík couldn't boast many buildings as charming as the old wooden house with its red walls, white window frames and little turret.

Her thoughts strayed to Sverrir. She assumed he was still in town and, now that it was the weekend, she might be able to invite him round for coffee. The interest was mutual, she could swear to it.

It was past seven o'clock and she was about to head

out to the restaurant when there was a knock at the door. The sound made her jump and for a moment she dithered, feeling trapped, afraid it was her mystery stalker – the unknown figure at the bathroom window, the silent caller . . . Was it a man or a woman? There was only one escape route from the flat, unless she tried to squeeze out of a window. Her imagination went into overdrive, her breathing ragged, her heart pounding.

There was another knock at the door, a little more peremptory than before. Tinna had never got round to putting in a doorbell, let alone an entryphone, and there was no peephole either, but then none of this had seemed necessary in a peaceful community like Akureyri. She had never felt insecure there before. But now the threat was almost palpable, and unnervingly close.

It occurred to her not to open the door, though it must be clear from the lights inside that someone was home. But then she told herself to get a grip; that she was probably overthinking the whole thing and that it was only an innocent visitor outside.

Bracing herself, she moved forwards and opened the door. Standing on the step was none other than Sverrir.

She could relax.

'Sverrir, hello,' she said, unable to hide her relief. 'Come in.'

'I wasn't intending to stay,' he replied, but he accepted her invitation nonetheless and followed her inside, where he took a seat on the sofa. 'I just wanted to check you were OK. And I've got an answer to that question you asked me.' There was a note in his voice that warned Tinna something was up.

She sat down herself, careful to maintain a discreet distance between them. She noted that he was casually dressed, and interpreted the fact as meaning that this was a courtesy call.

'Anyway, how are you?' he asked.

'I'm fine.'

'This must all have been a bit of a strain, I imagine?'

She paused and thought for a moment, then said: 'I think I can safely say that it hasn't been easy. It's been a very unsettling experience.'

'We're wrapping up the investigation,' he said, 'as you've probably guessed. It all appears pretty straightforward now. We don't actually know Fridjón's motive for attacking Yrsa, but that's not our biggest priority. What matters most is that the, er, danger has passed, if I can put it like that.' But Tinna could tell that he didn't entirely believe this claim himself.

'Yes, that's a huge relief.'

'Of course, there was probably never any danger to anyone else – apart from Yrsa, that is. Although we don't know what prompted Fridjón to do it, the bad blood was almost certainly a private matter between the two of them and didn't involve anyone else. He had no wife or children, and his only surviving family member is his brother, who lives here in the north but apparently had little contact with him. Even his friends seem to have known next to nothing about his private life.'

'Can I offer you something?' Tinna asked, taking advantage of this pause in his account.

Sverrir hesitated. 'Er, yes, maybe . . .'

'It's a bit late for coffee, don't you think? How about some red wine? Unless you're on duty, of course.'

'What? Oh, no. No, I'm not on duty now, so, yes, please. I wouldn't say no to a glass.'

Tinna got up and went into the kitchen, where she opened the only bottle of red wine she had – it was cheap plonk, but hopefully better than nothing. She poured two glasses.

'Thanks.' Sverrir took a sip. 'By the way, I heard back about that phone call. It's rather odd, actually.'

This gave her a nasty jolt, as she'd been praying there would be a perfectly natural explanation for the silent call.

'I'm sure it's nothing to worry about, though,' Sverrir added.

'Really?'

'Yes. The call was made from the sanatorium.'

'From the sanatorium?'

That late in the evening? No one should have been there at that hour. She shivered.

'Yes. Do you have any idea who it could have been?' he asked, and she got the impression that he wasn't entirely easy in his own mind that the mystery of the recent deaths had been satisfactorily solved. That he himself thought the solution had been just a bit too neat and tidy.

She thought fast, trying not to give anything away, concealing her fear. 'Actually, I do have an idea what's going on. An old incident – nothing to do with the recent events,' she lied, hoping he wouldn't see through her pretence.

'Ah, I see. Are you absolutely sure you don't want me to look into it for you?'

She shook her head. 'Are you certain the call came from the sanatorium?'

'Yes.'

'OK. Then no, it's all right. It's not a problem.'

All the same, she was grateful that he was there and she didn't have to digest this news alone. 'You're not in a hurry to be off, are you?' she asked.

'Er, no, no, not particularly,' he replied, a little embarrassed.

She leaned forwards in her seat, closer to him, and smelt the fragrance of his aftershave. Although he was informally dressed, his jacket and jeans were smart, as if he'd made an effort to look good. Perhaps he'd had an ulterior motive for this visit and the phone call had been no more than a pretext.

'You've got a nice flat here,' he said.

'Thank you.' She smiled. 'Whereabouts do you live – in Reykjavík, I mean?'

'Oh, I live on Snorrabraut. It's only a little bachelor pad, but it's all right.'

Bachelor pad, she noted. That was the key word.

'Would you like a snack with your wine?' she asked. 'I've got . . .' Damn, there was hardly anything in the kitchen. 'I've got some crackers, I think, and possibly some cheese.'

'That would be great.'

She got up again and went through to the kitchen, where she put together a rather meagre snack. Back in the sitting room, she laid the plate on the coffee table and sat down, this time seizing the chance to join Sverrir on the sofa, though still keeping a polite distance. She found his presence comfortable. For the first time in days, she felt safe.

'Akureyri's a nice town,' he said, after a brief silence.

'Yes, I grew up here, but, as it happens, I'm starting a new job soon in Reykjavík.' It didn't matter if she dressed up the truth slightly: the end justified the means.

'Seriously?' He brightened up. 'A nursing position, is it?'

'Yes, that's right.'

'Great. Then maybe we should meet up for coffee once you've moved.'

She smiled. 'I'd love to.'

Then, just for a second, a chill ran through her, as she realized belatedly that this man was a virtual stranger. But one thing she did know about him was that, as the officer in charge of the investigation, he must have a set of keys to the hospital. Come to think of it, she'd seen him opening the door one morning. Could he be the person who'd made the phone call? The figure lurking outside her window?

She tried to shrug off her sudden sense of disquiet.

2012

Helgi

Helgi was planning to track Tinna down at the City Hospital, where she worked. He knew he was straying into a grey area here, as an ordinary member of the public ambushing someone who had made it abundantly clear that she had no wish to talk to him. But he couldn't stop obsessing about the case; there was something there he couldn't put his finger on, some truth lurking just below the surface. Helgi the cop had gained the upper hand and Helgi the academic had been forced to take a back seat.

He had slept badly. He and Bergthóra had shared a bed, a sign that their relationship was returning to normal, though he knew the truce was only temporary; the problem hadn't gone away, though he tried not to dwell on the thought. He didn't have time for that right now. Last night, he had dreamt about Tinna. He had never met her, only read about her in the files, where he had also seen an old photo of her, but he had a hunch that she might hold a key to the mystery. So much for the promise he had made himself to approach this like any other assignment and not like an unsolved riddle. But then he had so often made himself promises, only to break them.

Helgi approached the grey-haired man at the hospital reception desk. 'I'm looking for one of your nurses, Tinna Einarsdóttir. Could you tell me which ward she works on?'

The man's face darkened. 'We don't give out information like that, I'm afraid,' he replied brusquely.

'I'm sorry. My name's Helgi Reykdal and I'm from the police.' He hadn't intended to play this card, but he reasoned with himself that it wasn't that far from the truth. He had as good as accepted the job offer from Magnús and could have started work in CID by now had he wanted to; it was only a question of formalities.

'Oh, sorry. Tinna, did you say? Just a minute, I need to look her up on here,' the man replied, fortunately not asking to see any ID.

'No rush,' Helgi said politely.

'She's up on the third floor,' the man announced after a moment, sounding much more amenable now. 'The lifts are over there on the right, then it's down the corridor and right again. I don't know if she's on duty, but they'll be able to tell you on the ward.'

Helgi followed his directions and asked for Tinna at the nursing station of the ward in question. 'Is Tinna around, by any chance?'

'Tinna? No, she's off sick today,' a middle-aged woman in a white coat answered him. 'Can I take a message?'

He thought fast. 'No, no, it's OK. I was just passing and wanted to say hello.'

The woman smiled.

Helgi wasn't about to give up so easily. His next stop would be Tinna's house. He might as well give it a final shot and try knocking on her door.

2012

Helgi

Tinna lived in an attractive terraced house in the suburb of Árbær, if the information in the online telephone directory was correct. It was a white, two-storey building and looked well maintained, every detail neatly finished, the garden full of trees and bushes, in keeping with the established, leafy neighbourhood.

Helgi walked up to the front door and rang the bell. There were lights in the windows on both floors, so clearly somebody was home.

He waited patiently and was finally rewarded with the sound of movement inside.

A man of around sixty opened the door. Helgi hadn't thought to read the names on the letterbox and, since the man was now blocking his view, he couldn't surreptitiously check to see who he was addressing.

'Good afternoon,' the man said guardedly, making no attempt to introduce himself. He evidently wasn't used to receiving visits at this time of day. The fact he was at home suggested he must be retired, though he gave the impression of being very fit.

'Yes, good afternoon. My name's Helgi Reykdal.'

The man nodded and muttered something inaudible, fixing Helgi with a fierce glare and waiting for his response. Helgi had the disconcerting feeling of having stumbled into the middle of a conversation without knowing what it was about or who he was talking to.

'I was trying to get hold of Tinna. Is she at home, by any chance?' Helgi made an effort to be as polite as possible in the face of this hostile reception.

'She's here, but she doesn't want to talk to you.'

Helgi was wrong-footed. 'Er, I'm sorry? . . . Why . . . ?'

'You rang her the other day, didn't you?'

Helgi nodded.

'As far as I'm aware, she made it perfectly clear then that she didn't want to talk to you,' the man continued, in a tone of barely suppressed rage.

Helgi felt like a naughty schoolboy summoned to the headteacher's office. He didn't know what to say.

The man hadn't finished: 'Then we'd appreciate it if you stopped bothering us, Helgi. My wife has nothing to say about that business, and I can't understand what you hope to achieve by harassing us like this. We're talking about something that happened in 1983, that everyone's forgotten about long ago. No one wants to have to rake up traumatic memories like that.'

'I'm sorry, it's just that I'm . . . I'm writing a dissertation about the case, that's all. I simply wanted to talk to the people who were there at the time and try to get a better idea of what went on.'

'All the same, you have to respect the fact that the people concerned might not want to talk to you.'

'Oh, absolutely, I do . . .' Helgi faltered. 'But I just thought I'd have another go.' He was ashamed of himself; his ambition had led him to cross a line. In retrospect, he realized he should have called it a day after his abortive phone conversation with Tinna, but this was a pattern of behaviour he recognized in himself; a tendency to become obsessed by a problem, so immersed in it that he got caught up in the detail and failed to see the bigger picture. 'I'm sorry,' he said. 'Please accept my sincere apologies for disturbing you.'

The man seemed slightly mollified. The tension in his face relaxed and he almost smiled. 'That's all right. I take it that means you won't be bothering us again. Anyway, good luck with your dissertation.'

'Thank you.'

'But I hope you don't have any crazy ideas about re-opening the investigation?' The sharp edge had returned to the man's voice.

'No, not exactly . . .' Helgi stammered.

'The case was closed, it was settled – there was no doubt about the conclusion,' the man said decisively. 'No doubt at all.' There was something odd about the way he phrased this, about his vehemence. He seemed almost unnaturally eager to leave the past undisturbed. Yet again Helgi had a powerful intuition that he needed to dig deeper.

'I agree,' he said disingenuously, keen to avoid any more unpleasantness for the moment.

The man nodded, as if they had just concluded some tricky negotiations in which Helgi had come off worst. Without any more ado, he shut the door, leaving Helgi standing there on the steps like an idiot.

He was so thrown by his reception that he almost forgot to check the names on the letterbox, but halfway to the gate, he remembered and turned back.

Sverrir Eggertsson and Tinna Einarsdóttir

It took him a second or two to twig.

Sverrir Eggertsson, the police officer who had been in charge of the investigation in Akureyri.

Did this mean that he had married a woman who had been a suspect at the time?

He had been at pains to stress that the case was closed and there was no reason to revisit it.

Could that have been motivated by a need to justify his own conclusions in the inquiry? To cover up his mistakes, even?

Or . . . did he have another, more dubious purpose still: that of protecting Tinna?

2012

Tinna

Tinna stirred and opened her eyes in the darkness of her bedroom. Her dreams had been infiltrated by unsettling memories of the long-ago events in Akureyri, so waking up was probably a blessing in disguise, though she often found it hard to drop off again. At least she felt comfortable here in their house in Árbær. It was where she and Sverrir had lived for nearly twenty years and brought up their only child, who now lived abroad. They envisaged staying here for a while longer, at least until she retired, perhaps even after that. There was a good atmosphere in the house, nothing to remind her of the terrible events that had brought her and Sverrir together, and often many days would pass without her thoughts turning to the past. But now it seemed that her time at the sanatorium had crept back into her subconscious, thanks to that bloody young man who was writing a dissertation about the deaths and wouldn't leave them alone.

Yes, she was happy here. But even so, when Sverrir was away she missed his comforting presence beside her and sometimes managed to frighten herself silly over nothing, like a small child. At those times the mysterious phone call and the unexplained prowler outside her flat in Akureyri thirty years ago would come back to haunt her. The memories were still so vivid that she could almost relive them moment by moment, as if fear had intensified the experiences and etched them indelibly on her mind and soul. It had been then, at the lowest point in her life, that Sverrir had entered the picture, first as her protector, then as an excuse to uproot herself and move to Reykjavík. It hadn't taken them long to make that decision after their first night together at her flat.

Although she had never again experienced anything like that uncanny night-time visit and phone call, the anxiety still returned to haunt her. The unsettling incidents had abruptly ceased after she and Sverrir got together, but every now and then, usually in the early hours when her unconscious mind was in charge, she allowed herself to wonder whether Sverrir himself could have played some part in those events. Could he have been watching her? Had he tried to peer in at her window and made that phone call to her? Could she have walked straight into his trap?

At other times, she had a crawling sensation that she was still being watched.

She wasn't sure what had woken her now, unless it had been the awareness of Sverrir's absence. Could she have heard a noise? She had a vague feeling that she had in the depths of her dreams, but she wasn't quite sure, so she sat up and listened.

It was a year since Sverrir had left the police. To supplement his income, he'd taken a part-time job as a nightwatchman. He was in very good shape and earned quite a generous amount from taking a few night shifts on top of his police pension, but Tinna was finding it hard to get used to sleeping alone, and her rest was always fitful on those nights when he was working.

All was quiet in the house, yet she felt a prickle of unease, and all of a sudden she was transported back thirty years to her flat in Akureyri, as alone and vulnerable as she had been then. It was the same feeling, a piercing terror that she wasn't alone and someone was watching her, though the idea was absurd. She was in the upstairs bedroom of their house and there was no way anyone could be outside the window. Of course there was nobody watching her.

But then she remembered what it was that had woken her, mingling with her dream or nightmare. It was the sound of the front door, the familiar sound of a key being inserted into the lock. But that wasn't possible, it just wasn't possible. Sverrir was at work, wasn't he? Then it came back to her with a jolt that she had lost her house keys two days ago. Or perhaps not lost but mislaid them and now couldn't remember where she'd put them. It was always happening. They must be somewhere in the house. The fact hadn't bothered her unduly until now that she was alone.

Was it possible that Sverrir had come home early for

some reason and didn't want to disturb her . . . ? Perhaps he was in the kitchen, having a quiet snack. She smiled at the thought. It occurred to her to call down to him, but somehow she couldn't bring herself to do it. She tried to convince herself that she was imagining things, that she hadn't been woken by the noise of the front door but just happened to have stirred, and that the sensible thing would be to lie down again, close her eyes and go back to sleep. After all, she had been ill with flu and needed her rest.

She strained her ears but couldn't detect any sounds beyond the hissing of the radiators and the normal night noises of the house. The thought of the missing keys nagged at her, though. Supposing somebody had stolen them? Would she have the strength to defend herself against an assailant?

Tinna did her best to push away these paranoid imaginings. She was as safe as could be, she told herself, at home in the Reykjavík suburbs. Of course there wasn't an intruder in the house.

Come to think of it, some of the parquet blocks on the landing were a bit loose and creaked when anyone trod on them. She'd been pestering Sverrir to take them up and fix them properly, but these little chores tended to be put on the back burner. Since he'd retired, Sverrir seemed to have less free time than ever; as well as getting a night job, he'd become an enthusiastic golfer, met up regularly with friends and old colleagues, and had even taken up the guitar. Bless him, he seemed thirty years younger, in spirit at least, since giving up work.

What a good thing he hadn't got round to fixing those loose parquet blocks, she told herself, because no burglar would be able to get near the bedroom without treading on them and giving their presence away.

The thought made her feel a little easier in her mind.

She could afford to relax.

Lying back on her pillow, she pulled her duvet up to her chin to dispel her shivers.

How ridiculous to give way to such absurd ideas in the middle of the night.

If she had any sense, she would concentrate on getting back to sleep as quickly as possible, since she was thinking of going in to work for the morning shift tomorrow, now that she was feeling a lot better from her flu.

She reached an arm out from under the duvet and grabbed her phone from the bedside table to check the time; it wasn't even two yet. Only an hour and a half since Sverrir had left for work. She wasn't used to waking up at this time of night. Perhaps there had been a noise outside – people on their way home from clubbing in town, for example, although the street was usually very peaceful.

Should she maybe ring Sverrir, just to hear the sound of his voice?

No, there was no reason to call him, and it would only make her even more wakeful.

Noticing that her phone had almost run out of battery, she got out of bed and plugged it into the charger on the floor in the corner. Then she scurried back into the warmth under the duvet.

All was quiet, and she felt her body relaxing as she began to look forward to going back to work tomorrow and to seeing Sverrir at breakfast. He usually fried eggs and bacon when he came off his night shift and treated her to breakfast with hot coffee and orange juice. One of life's great pleasures.

Tinna wriggled into a more comfortable position and closed her eyes.

It was then that she heard the creak on the landing.

The familiar noise seared through flesh and bone. She stiffened up, lying there rigid with terror, unable to move a muscle, feeling her heart go into overdrive and the sweat breaking out all over her body. Her eyes were wide open, but she couldn't see much in the dark. The door was slightly ajar. Should she leap out of bed and close it? It had no lock, so that wouldn't achieve much. Should she dash over to the corner and grab her phone? Would she have time to do one or both things? The thoughts flashed through her head at the speed of light, yet the seconds seemed to be passing like minutes.

It must be Sverrir. There could be no other explanation. He must have had to leave early for some reason – perhaps he'd got his days mixed up and wasn't supposed to be on duty. Or he'd caught her flu and come home because he was feeling out of sorts. Yes, that must be it. Of course. She'd thought he seemed a bit under the weather earlier. Poor love.

Feeling reassured, she called out: 'Sverrir? Sverrir? Are you back?' She could hear the tremor in her voice. 'Darling, is that you?'

No answer.

Why the hell wasn't he answering?

The blood seemed to freeze in her veins. She tried to call out to her husband again, but the words died in her throat. All she knew was that there was somebody on the landing and it wasn't Sverrir. She was overwhelmed by a suffocating sense of panic, the old memories of the figure outside her window returning with a vengeance. But this time she was totally defenceless; there was nothing between her and the intruder but thin air.

And she had given away her presence by calling out like that . . .

She lay paralysed with fear under the duvet, waiting for the inevitable.

In the gloom she saw the bedroom door begin to open wider . . .

2012

Helgi

All was sweetness and light again. Helgi and Bergthóra had talked things over and agreed to carry on working through their problems and strengthening their relationship. Privately, Helgi wasn't actually sure they had a future together, but that problem was better ignored for now. He needed to knuckle down and finish his dissertation, so he could graduate from his MA course, then get himself established with the police. He was more or less resigned now to accepting the position with Reykjavík CID.

They had eaten breakfast together – porridge, like every weekday morning. He wasn't that into porridge himself, but Bergthóra had grown up with it, so that was how it was to be in their household too. She decided this, as she did most things, it seemed to him. But that was fine; it made sense not to sweat the small stuff.

They had originally met at a mutual friend's wedding.

Her enigmatic smile and distant gaze had captivated him from the first. The physical attraction had been instant and powerful. That hadn't changed. And she was super bright, too; he had seen that straight away. They'd soon found themselves talking away whole evenings and nights. Everything had gone smoothly at first, and before he knew it he had fallen in love. He was still in love, in spite of everything. She was someone who knew her own mind and could be uncompromising at times, but in a way he respected this.

He was sitting alone at the kitchen table, listening to the radio, on which the midday news was about to begin. He had spent the morning writing and his work had been progressing quite well. Perhaps his bad conscience over his decision to doorstep Tinna had had a motivating effect on him.

Lunch was a delicious bowl of Icelandic *skyr.* Bergthóra wasn't a fan of dairy products so he tended to indulge himself when she wasn't home.

After lunch, he meant to enjoy a bit of alone time, select another novel from the shelves and read for a while. He had his eye on one he hadn't read for years, probably not since he was fourteen or fifteen, a battered old paperback called *Enter a Murderer*, the only Icelandic translation of a work by Ngaio Marsh, New Zealand's queen of crime. The book had fond associations for him, like so many volumes in the collection; he clearly remembered reading the last chapters during a shopping trip he'd made with his mother as a child. He'd had no interest in what they were buying but had found himself a bench and sat down with the book, losing himself in a classic murder mystery set in the theatre world. In the intervening years, he had read many other books by Marsh – perhaps all of them – but he had never reread this one and could recall almost nothing of the plot. He yearned to lose himself in its pages, returning not only to the mystery but to his childhood, when everything had been so much simpler. Because nothing was simple any more. There were so many decisions weighing on him, yet at the same time it felt as if they had been taken out of his hands. He had resolved to see things through because that's what Bergthóra wanted. He was going to accept the job with the police because that's what she wanted. The idea that he had any say himself was an illusion, pure fantasy. But at least there were some areas where he had the whip hand. He knew he would be good at his job, that he would be a decent police officer, or at least a promising one. This type of work appealed to him and he was looking forward to the new challenge. The police was his world, free from Bergthóra's interference. And his books – they were a refuge too. The same could be said of his dissertation, though he blew hot and cold in his attitude to that. Some days he found it grindingly tedious; other days the cold case exerted a powerful hold on him. It infuriated him that he couldn't grasp the big picture; that an essential piece of the puzzle seemed to be missing.

Hell, it couldn't be helped.

The *skyr* was good anyway. He'd missed proper Icelandic *skyr* when he was living abroad. Yoghurt just wasn't the same.

They were playing the final song before the radio news. This time it was performed by a male-voice choir, and the sound took Helgi back to family meals long ago. They all used to sit over lunch, listening to the news, with rye bread and *skyr* on the table, and traditional pickled whey to drink. At the time, he'd been bored by the routineness of it all, but now in his memories this had come to seem like a symbol of security and permanence. He was conscious that he was deliberately indulging his nostalgia every day by listening to Icelandic National Radio, eating *skyr* for lunch and reading the old books. It all pointed to the same thing: a longing for the security of the past, a need for reassurance in a world that felt anything but safe, in a home where he had never experienced the same peace as he had in his parents' house. Perhaps, deep down, he just wanted to work in a bookshop instead of playing at being a cop, however much aptitude he might show for the job.

'A woman in her fifties was found dead at her home in Árbær this morning. The police have not released any details so far, but, according to news sources, the matter is being investigated as a possible murder.'

The first item in the midday news round-up jolted Helgi out of his thoughts. His initial response was a natural feeling of dismay, coupled perhaps with the instinctive reaction of a policeman. A murder in Reykjavík: that certainly wasn't an everyday occurrence.

But then, a few seconds later, the newsreader's words sank in.

A woman in her fifties.

Árbær.

Shit.

It wasn't possible.

It had to be a coincidence.

His first impulse was to ring her just to be sure, but he hesitated. Her husband's message had been pretty unequivocal yesterday.

Helgi scraped back his chair and leapt to his feet, almost knocking over his *skyr* in his agitation. He fetched his laptop and opened the main news outlets, but there was no other information about the case, just the same bald facts; no pictures from the scene. To give the media their due, they were capable of showing discretion at times like this.

It occurred to him to ring Magnús, his prospective boss, or drop by the police station and try to glean more information that way, but he would rather not. The chances that the woman was Tinna were vanishingly small, and he didn't want to make a fool of himself at his new office before he'd even started work there.

The rest of the news headlines passed unheeded. He'd lost his appetite for the *skyr.* For once, he couldn't face reading a novel either. He resolved to get back to the computer and try to make some progress on his dissertation.

2012

Hulda

There were several cases on Hulda's desk that morning, but nothing urgent. In fact, she'd got the feeling over the last few months that Magnús was sparing her all the complicated jobs. 'Sparing' probably wasn't the right word. In reality, she felt as if the more challenging cases were being systematically withheld from her. It hadn't always been like that, though her career in the police had felt like a constant uphill battle against the patriarchy. At least she used to be trusted with major cases, even with high-profile ones, though no honours had ever accompanied the successes she had achieved, often against the odds. But recently something had changed. It was her last year in the job, and she supposed Magnús's decision to pass her over could partly be blamed on that, were it not for her belief that her status had been deteriorating steadily ever since Magnús took over as her boss. The last in a long series of male bosses, almost none of them as talented as her – in her opinion, at least.

Although she didn't belong to the boys' club and was rarely the first to hear the station gossip, it didn't take long for the news to filter through to her that the wife of a former colleague had been murdered.

Details were frustratingly thin on the ground, but there was no hiding the fact that Sverrir Eggertsson, who had retired the previous year, was at this moment being interviewed by his former colleagues. Reading the mood at the station, she inferred that he was a suspect. That in itself would be a matter of great embarrassment to the police, who were presumably at pains to stop the news leaking out. Everyone would be hoping that Sverrir hadn't been involved and could be eliminated from the list of suspects as soon as possible. Hulda knew him reasonably well, having worked with him more than once over the years, though she had never established a particularly close relationship with him. Inevitably, he had a lot of mates in CID, so it would be hard to find anyone neutral to question him.

It so happened that Hulda had also been acquainted with the murder victim. She remembered Tinna pretty clearly from meeting her in Akureyri during one of the more unsettling cases she could remember working on, which would still be listed as unsolved if it had been left up to her. Or perhaps she'd have been able to solve it herself if Sverrir hadn't got in the way. He had jumped at a straightforward solution when it was offered, and, as if that wasn't bad enough, he'd been spotted in Tinna's company shortly after the investigation had ended. Hulda had found this irregular, not to mention inappropriate, but their colleagues had been reluctant to make an issue out of it. They'd dismissed the problem by saying that love could blossom in the unlikeliest of circumstances. And, to be fair, the investigation had been formally closed by that stage and Tinna hadn't been a suspect.

Hulda had subsequently seen her at police socials over the years, though she herself had pretty much stopped attending them since losing her husband. Tinna, who'd always been glamorous, had aged well. She and Sverrir had appeared happy together. Although Sverrir could be overbearing to the point of rudeness at work and in his dealings with Hulda, she'd nevertheless sensed that he was a decent man at heart, a good husband. It seemed unthinkable that he could have suddenly resorted to killing his wife after three decades of marriage.

Hulda refused to believe it, though she had learnt during her long career never to rule anything out. In the unlikely event that he was guilty, she thought, was there any chance that his action could have had its roots in the old case . . . ?

Hulda sat at her desk, staring at the piles of papers, turning the problem over in her mind, letting her thoughts drift back to 1983.

No one had come to speak to her this morning, not even to pick her brains, and certainly not to invite her to become formally involved in the investigation. Things weren't like they used to be, though she was still of the opinion that she was one of the best detectives on the team. Age hadn't affected her performance much. She might not be on top of all the latest investigative methods, but she knew how to separate the wheat from the chaff and tease out the truth.

Just because her superiors had stopped turning to her for the big cases, that didn't mean she herself had any intention of throwing in the towel – not yet, at any rate. Making a sudden decision, she got up and strode purposefully down the corridor in the direction of Magnús's office.

When she rapped on the glass, she saw him glance up from his computer with a look of surprise. He lowered his eyes to his screen again as if he was going to pretend he hadn't noticed her standing there, but in the end he gestured at her to come in. She opened the door and stepped into the office, which was a lot more spacious than her own, but then that was hardly surprising, seeing as Magnús was head of department. It was a seat she would have given anything to warm herself, but that hadn't happened and now it never would.

'Magnús,' she said politely.

'Yes? Look, I'm a bit pressed for time,' he answered curtly, eyes glued to his screen again.

'It's about Sverrir . . .'

'Yes?' he repeated.

'Sverrir and Tinna, the woman who was found murdered—'

This time he looked up and interrupted before she could continue. 'I know all about it, Hulda.'

'I used to work with him, including on the case in

Akureyri where he and Tinna met. I was just wondering if I could help at all, join the investigation and take . . .'

Magnús stared at her as if she had said something incomprehensible.

Then, after a brief pause, he replied: 'There's no need for that. We've already got enough people working on it, thanks all the same.'

His gaze returned to his computer screen in an unmistakable signal that the conversation was over.

2012

Helgi

The day had passed without any further updates about the death in Árbær. For some reason, the police were refusing to disclose any more details.

Helgi had managed to develop a number of his notes for his dissertation, though Tinna was constantly in his thoughts. He tried to tell himself that it was all in his imagination and that Tinna was perfectly fine. He couldn't believe how anxious he was feeling about a woman he'd never even met. At least some of this had to be down to guilt; the fear that if something had happened to her, it might be partly his fault. Had he turned over too many stones in the course of his digging?

Wrenching his mind away from Tinna and back to his work, he paused to consider the notes he had written following his conversation with Elísabet. There had been an air of sadness about her, as if she hadn't led a happy life and was still lost in a fog of discontent. He had a hunch that she hadn't been telling him the whole truth. But then how could he expect a complete stranger to open up to him without reservation?

Helgi took out his phone and selected her number. He just had to talk to someone about the case. There was no point trying to get hold of Tinna again, and he was reluctant to talk to Broddi. The former caretaker was all too eager to unburden, to pour out his depressing hard-luck stories. As for Thorri, Helgi had zero desire to speak to him again unless there was no alternative. A genuinely odd guy whose manner was anything but charming.

'Yes . . . hello?' Although the voice was friendly, Helgi thought Elísabet sounded wary.

'Hello, Elísabet. Helgi Reykdal here. I hope you don't mind me bothering you for a minute?'

'Oh, no, of course not, no problem.'

'You see, I'm putting the finishing touches to my dissertation and I just wanted to double-check the information I got from you and your former colleagues at the sanatorium.'

'Have you spoken to everyone?' she asked.

'Yes, I think so.'

'Thorri too?' she asked, somewhat unexpectedly, since it had been fairly obvious when they spoke that Thorri was no favourite of hers.

'Yes, I went to see him at his clinic.'

'Ah, right, here in town, you mean. I gather he's making a pretty good living from that,' she said, with a note in her voice that might have been resentment.

'You said when we met that you two hadn't got on that well together?'

There was a pause, then she said: 'No, we didn't get on.'

'You mentioned that he wasn't a good manager. Were there any other question marks over his work?' Helgi asked. It was a shot in the dark, prompted by his own misgivings about the doctor.

Another pause. 'No, no, he was a decent doctor. It was, well, personal.'

'Ah, I see,' he said after a moment. 'Was there any particular reason for that?'

Elísabet was silent for a while, then replied: 'Just personal, like I said.' But after a moment she elaborated: 'I suppose you could say it was because of an affair that came to nothing.'

Her honesty took Helgi by surprise. Surely she must have been married back then, given that she'd only recently lost her husband?

'Let's keep that between ourselves,' she added. 'Nothing ever happened. You won't mention it in your dissertation, will you?'

'No, of course not.'

'Have you spoken to Tinna as well?' she asked, obviously keen to change the subject.

'Well, only briefly. On the phone. I didn't get to meet her. I don't think she wanted to talk to me.'

'I expect you've realized by now that she married Sverrir, the police officer in charge of the investigation?'

'Yes, I've met him,' Helgi replied. 'I can't say he gave me a very warm welcome.'

'I was going to tell you when we met the other day, but I had second thoughts. I don't like to gossip, but it came as a shock to the rest of us at the time. Rather irregular, don't you think? He'd been investigating a murder case that Tinna was involved in – not just involved in but a potential suspect. Not exactly professional behaviour, was it?' From her scandalized tone, it was clear that, in spite of her protests, Elísabet loved nothing more than a good gossip.

'Unusual, certainly.'

'I believe they got together while the inquiry was still in progress. That's what the rumours said, anyway. That they'd started seeing each other while he was in Akureyri working on the case. It didn't take her long to up sticks and move south to join him in Reykjavík afterwards.'

'Do you think there could have been anything more to it than just . . . well, two people falling in love?' Helgi asked.

'Meaning what?'

'Well, do you think he could have been covering up for her in some way?'

'Naturally, the thought had crossed my mind,' Elísabet answered, rather sharply. 'Who knows? Not that I mean to claim that Tinna had anything to do with Yrsa's murder – that would be hard to picture . . .'

'Yes, it would,' Helgi agreed, and waited for Elísabet to continue.

'But . . . but we shouldn't forget that she was the one who found both bodies,' she went on, and it was obvious that she had considered the question before and no doubt discussed her theory many times over the years. 'Both bodies! That's a pretty strange coincidence, don't you think?'

'Actually, I understand from the police reports that she always arrived first in the mornings, so perhaps it wasn't such a coincidence.'

'The police reports that Sverrir wrote?'

'Er, yes, sure, I suppose. But you said yourself that she always got in first.'

'Well, yes. I mean, it's true that she usually got in before the rest of us.'

'Still, it's certainly worth considering,' Helgi said. 'Of course, I'm not intending to go into the content of the case in that much depth or cast doubt on the police's findings at the time, but this does provide an interesting bit of background information.'

'I should think so. Maybe you'd let me read your dissertation one day? And don't hesitate to get in touch if there's anything else I can help you with. I'm free for coffee any time,' she said, and he didn't doubt the truth of this last statement.

After watching the evening news on both channels, Helgi was still none the wiser about the death in Árbær. He and Bergthóra had eaten a rather bland poached haddock for supper at around six, according to their unvarying routine. They hadn't spoken much during the meal, though she had nagged him yet again about formally accepting the position with the police.

'You can't keep messing around like this, and, besides,

we could do with the additional money in our household kitty,' she said, taking a sip of water. They always had water with supper. 'You can't just live off your study loan; you'll only accumulate more debt.'

'I'm fine for now, Bergthóra.'

'Yes, sure, but we could do with the extra income if we want to buy somewhere and not be stuck renting for ever. I've been looking at flats on various websites. There's quite a lot on offer.'

'Well, I'm not so sure this is the right time,' Helgi said. 'Shouldn't we wait and see if the prices drop a little further? We don't want our mortgage to shoot up as soon as there's a hike in inflation.' He felt a little guilty saying this, remembering the economist on the radio predicting a steep rise in property prices, but he simply wasn't ready to take this step yet. Not with Bergthóra.

2012

Elísabet

She sat at the kitchen table, staring at her mobile phone and worrying that she might have said too much to Helgi. It had just been so nice to talk to someone, and he had such a pleasant voice. She'd felt instinctively that she could trust him, that he wouldn't betray her.

Thorri . . . It was years since she had last spoken to him, and although she'd occasionally spotted him around and about in Akureyri, she hadn't attempted to approach him. But she'd kept an eye on him from a distance. His private clinic in Reykjavík seemed to be doing very nicely, as far as she could see.

Their flirtation at work had been an embarrassing episode, over almost before it had begun, yet she still thought about it even now. He had come on to her at the end of a staff party, despite knowing that she was married, or perhaps because he'd known that her marriage was an unhappy one. She supposed everyone had noticed, since gossip spread like wildfire in a small town like Akureyri. Yet she had stuck by her husband all these years, first for her son's sake, then out of habit, because she didn't know any other life and didn't have the courage or energy to leave. People could get used to anything. The upshot was that she hadn't gained her freedom until her husband died last year, at which point she had finally gathered the momentum to uproot herself and move south to Reykjavík for a fresh start. But the sad truth was that she had never been lonelier.

Although the attraction had been mutual, Elísabet had rejected Thorri's advances that first evening, out of a reluctance to cheat on her husband. For days afterwards she hadn't been able to think about anything else. It had taken her a week to summon up the courage to tell Thorri how she really felt, a week during which she had convinced herself that she was ready to break up with her husband, walk out of her marriage and embark on a new life with Thorri.

But when she finally opened her heart to him, he had reacted by humiliating her.

'You didn't seriously think I meant anything by it?' he had asked coldly, a sarcastic sneer on his lips, his manner icy.

From that moment on she had turned against him. It had been a huge relief when he eventually transferred to the County Hospital, but despite that she had gone on grabbing every opportunity she could to badmouth him behind his back.

And she'd continued to keep tabs on him from a distance, much as she hated him.

On reflection, it had probably been a mistake to tell Helgi about their affair and plant the idea in his mind that she might not be an entirely neutral witness. She had the feeling that Helgi was intending to do more than simply write a dissertation about the deaths at the sanatorium. From his questions, she got the impression that he was taking a fresh look at the facts of the case, and, if so, it would probably have been more cunning of her to go on slandering Thorri. That would have given Helgi a reason to put him at the top of his list of suspects.

2012

Helgi

Tinna's name was published in the papers the following morning.

Although Helgi had been half prepared for the news, it still came as a shock to him. He had got up at the crack of dawn to fetch the papers and now, desperate to tell someone, he shook Bergthóra awake.

'The woman who was murdered in Árbær – she's the woman I was trying to talk to for my dissertation.'

Bergthóra opened her eyes but didn't look particularly amused to be disturbed from a deep sleep. 'Mm? So? What time is it, anyway?'

'Half past six, but didn't you hear what I said? The woman who was murdered – she was linked to the cold case in Akureyri. It could have been something I did that led to this . . .' The words came out in a rush and he could feel his heart pounding.

'Darling, I'm still half asleep,' Bergthóra protested. 'Do leave me alone. I'm sure it's just a coincidence.'

'But it can't be a coincidence, Bergthóra. Not now, when I've been . . .'

She closed her eyes and rolled over, turning her back to him. 'Oh, do let me sleep, Helgi.'

2012

Hulda

Hulda was determined not to let Magnús's brush-off the previous day get to her. She had several cases on the go and decided to concentrate on those: other people could take care of Sverrir and the murder investigation. But that hadn't stopped her from casting her mind back to 1983 and the deaths at the Akureyri sanatorium. Of course, her memories were hazy after so many years, but it had been the kind of investigation you didn't easily forget, particularly the grisly detail about poor Yrsa having her fingers cut off. The weapon used for her mutilation had never been found. Nor had they ever uncovered a motive.

Hulda began automatically to jot down a few points relating to the events, including all the names she could recall.

She remembered Broddi vividly. She'd never quite got a handle on him, finding him a little menacing at times, despite being moved by his plight. He had been like a man haunted by some mysterious sorrow. Sverrir had been far too quick to throw him in the cells – only one of a number of mistakes he'd made. He'd also been over-eager to close the case when the hospital director had turned up dead. It had been far too neat a solution in Hulda's view, but as so often – both then and later – she hadn't been given enough of a say in the investigation. Hadn't been in a position to make her objections heard.

Of course, she'd also met Tinna several times – the young woman who'd discovered both bodies. That was a troubling coincidence, Hulda thought, though there could have been a natural explanation for it. All the same, there was no denying that there had been a spark between Tinna and Sverrir during the investigation. Hulda hadn't failed to pick up on the chemistry between them at the time, but even so she had been rather taken aback – and she wasn't the only one – when they'd got together with what seemed like indecent haste after the inquiry ended. Yet, in spite of this, Hulda had never suspected Sverrir of any misconduct: if the evidence had suggested that Tinna had committed murder, he would unquestionably have arrested her. Though, granted, it had been a much easier decision to arrest Broddi. Sometimes Hulda had got the impression that everyone wanted Broddi to be guilty, as that would be the simplest, most convenient solution.

She remembered Fridjón too, the director of the sanatorium, who had died in a fall. It had never once entered her head that he could have been responsible for Yrsa's death. He'd been a sedate and self-possessed bachelor in his late sixties, a doctor of the old school, who seemed to carry the burden of all the world's sorrows on his shoulders. Even if his death was suicide, she thought, that didn't necessarily mean it should be read as a confession. And if it wasn't suicide, that meant there had been not one but two murders at the sanatorium. Yet Sverrir had concluded that Fridjón was the killer, and there had been no compelling evidence to prove him wrong, though Hulda would certainly have kept the case open longer if it had been up to her.

If and *would have* . . . it was always the same story when she thought back over her career. Admittedly, she had got to lead some major investigations in her time, but there was no question that many things would have been done differently if she'd enjoyed more support over the years.

Hulda thought back to the sanatorium case again. There had been another woman; she'd forgotten her name but she could still picture her. She'd come across as aloof, brusque and rather evasive, as though she hadn't been telling the whole truth, whether consciously or not. Yet it was hard to picture her in the role of a murderer and almost impossible to visualize her cutting the fingers off the woman she worked with. Somebody had done it, though, macabre and incomprehensible as it seemed. And if Hulda had learnt one thing over her long career, it was never to rule out anyone or anything.

Then there was the other doctor, Thorri. She remembered him clearly as well, not least as he had cropped up in the news from time to time over the intervening years, first as director of the County Hospital in Akureyri, then later as a spokesman for private practice in health care as well. A tall, good-looking, strongly built man who would no doubt have been physically capable of carrying out murder. He certainly couldn't be ruled out as a suspect, she thought. He'd had a cold, stand-offish manner. Whenever she saw him on the news, she was reminded of the deaths at the sanatorium and the same thought flashed through her head: could he have done it? Yet she had no idea what motive he could have had for killing Yrsa; she didn't even have any theories. All of which pointed to failings in the original inquiry; they just hadn't dug deep enough. Come to think of it, she recalled that there was one detail she would have liked to explore in more depth. Someone had alluded to Thorri's past during an interview with her and Sverrir, and hinted that he'd got into some kind of trouble in his previous job. Sverrir, however, had seen no reason to follow up this lead. And after that the inquiry had abruptly taken a different turn with Fridjón's death. Hulda wrote down Thorri's name, underlined it several times, then added: '*Previous job??*'

Though what was she intending to do about it now?

No, there was no point even thinking about it.

She laid aside the piece of paper. After all, it was nothing but a handful of names and a few scrawled notes.

She wouldn't waste any more time on it.

2012

Helgi

Helgi arrived at the police station on Hverfisgata at ten. As he approached the building, he found himself looking with new eyes at the modernist box, its frontage dominated by long rows of windows, that had been such a Reykjavík landmark since the 1960s. It was strange to think of himself working there.

He hadn't rung ahead, but he went over and introduced himself to the officer on reception and asked if he could see Magnús.

'I'll let him know you're here, but I can't guarantee he'll be available straight away,' the man told him.

Helgi could wait. It would allow him to put off the inevitable for a few more minutes – postpone the formal acceptance of the job he didn't particularly want to do. He had come here to say yes to Magnús's offer and, if possible, to pick up some more detailed information about Tinna and Sverrir. After this meeting with Magnús, all his dreams of working abroad would be shelved for good. He supposed the next step would be to give in to Bergthóra's wishes and move out of their rented place, plunging themselves into a sea of debt by investing in a flat somewhere on the outskirts of Reykjavík. That young economist on the radio had better be right about the trend in property prices.

After fifteen minutes, Helgi's name was called.

'Magnús is free now.'

He nodded and stood up. The waiting room was packed, and he had been passing the time by trying to guess the reason for each person's presence and why anyone would need to visit a police station in the middle of the day.

'He's on the third floor.'

Helgi went through the door indicated and took the old lift upstairs. The building was showing its age, yet its 1960s decor held a certain charm for him. He thought he might actually enjoy working here. It would be just as well if he did.

Once upstairs, he was shown into Magnús's office.

'Helgi, great to see you. Sorry to keep you waiting. Things are at fever pitch here, so I don't have much time.' Magnús had got to his feet and now came forward to shake Helgi by the hand. Then he said again: 'Great to see you.'

'Yeah, sorry to turn up without any warning like this.'

'No problem. Do sit down. Would you like a coffee?'

Magnús resumed his own seat behind his desk.

'Thanks.' Helgi took a chair facing him. 'And no, thanks – I'm good. I've already had a coffee this morning.'

'I assume you're here to discuss the job. I got the feeling last time we spoke that you'd more or less made up your mind to join us.' Magnús smiled.

'Ah, yes, sure . . . or . . .'

'You're not going to change your mind, are you, Helgi?' Magnús asked, his voice still friendly. 'The chair's practically waiting for you to fill it. One of my team is due to retire, and you have such outstanding references, both from your old colleagues here and from your tutor abroad. He said he'd never had such a brilliant student.'

Helgi, who hadn't been aware of this praise, couldn't help feeling gratified.

'Er, no, I haven't changed my mind, not at all, and yes, I have come here to deal with the formalities, but . . .'

'Fantastic, fantastic. I'm happy to hear that.'

'But there's something else I'd like to have a word about at the same time . . .'

'Sure, fire away.' Magnús leaned forward over his desk.

'It's about the woman who was found dead in Árbær.'

'Oh? Tinna, you mean?'

'Yes. The thing is, I was round there the day before she died – at her house.'

'You what? How come?' Magnús looked genuinely taken aback.

'The dissertation I'm writing – my MA dissertation – is concerned with the deaths that occurred at the Akureyri sanatorium in 1983. I'm reviewing the investigation from a criminological perspective, if you see what I mean?'

'Right . . .'

'So I've been researching the background to the case

and talking to the people involved. They're all still alive – or rather *were* still alive – and I've managed to speak to everyone except Tinna. I tried going round to her house in Árbær, but her husband answered the door to me and more or less threw me off the premises, saying that Tinna didn't want to talk about it. There wasn't much I could say to that. Then I learnt that the guy had been in charge of the investigation at the time . . .'

'Sverrir – yes, he was.' Magnús's face was grave now. 'That's interesting, Helgi, very interesting. Between you and me, Sverrir is the main suspect for his wife's murder at this stage, but it sounds as if it would be worth having a word with Tinna's former colleagues too . . . Needless to say, we're hoping there's another angle to this, because it would be gutting to have to charge a former police officer with murder. Nobody here believes that Sverrir's guilty, but right now he's the only suspect we're interviewing.'

'Is . . . er . . . is there anything to suggest he killed Tinna?' Helgi enquired, a little hesitantly, unsure how much it was appropriate for him to ask about the investigation. He found Magnús hard to read.

'Yes and no,' Magnús answered, apparently unfazed by the question. 'It's a relatively short time since he retired from the police, and he's been working shifts as a nightwatchman since then. He was on duty the night Tinna was murdered.'

'Isn't that enough to eliminate him?' Helgi asked.

'Well, we've established that he went to work and clocked in, but, as far as we can see, there's no way of ruling out the possibility that he slipped away at some point. And although there are two CCTV cameras, their evidence isn't conclusive either, as they don't cover all the exits from the building. So it's conceivable that he went to work, then sneaked off home shortly afterwards, returning later to finish his shift and clock out . . . An appalling thought, unthinkable really, but that's all we've got to work with so far.'

'And has he . . . well, has he said anything to indicate that he's guilty?'

'Absolutely not. He seems devastated and flatly denies having had anything to do with it. I'm inclined to give him the benefit of the doubt, but we're still questioning him. It would be great if you could join the investigation and lend us a hand by having another chat with the people you're already in contact with.'

Helgi was a little taken aback by this.

'But I . . . I've still got to finish my dissertation. I hadn't envisaged starting straight away.'

'Naturally you'd be given an opportunity to finish your studies, don't worry about that, but I think this would be an excellent time for you to start work here – straight in at the deep end, so to speak.'

'I'll certainly think about it, but . . . er . . .'

'There's nothing to think about,' Magnús said flatly. 'We'll do it like this – it'd be best for everyone.'

Helgi nodded, resigned to this fait accompli. Things hadn't gone quite as he'd intended, but there was no denying that he was tempted by the idea of being able to investigate the case with a police ID in his pocket. It would give him a real chance to winkle out the truth about those deaths thirty years ago. He was pretty sure that Tinna's murder was no coincidence but linked somehow to the past.

'Yes, well, maybe you're right; I should jump in at the deep end.' Helgi smiled. 'I'll . . . I'll get straight on to it. I've got a good office set-up at home.'

'Don't be ridiculous, you can work from here. Starting tomorrow. I've got a room all lined up for you; I just need to sort out the departure of the woman who's occupying it at present. Come and see me at the same time tomorrow and I'll show you the office. The salary will be the same as originally discussed.'

'Sounds good. I'll come by tomorrow morning then, and—'

'And get talking to your contacts straight away. We can't afford to waste any time in a major investigation like this.'

2012

Helgi

Helgi considered ringing Bergthóra first to tell her the good news – well, the news. It still hadn't sunk in and he couldn't make up his mind whether it was a positive move for him or not.

Instead of calling her, he selected Thorri's number. He wanted to catch the doctor before he went back to Akureyri, assuming he hadn't already left.

'Yes,' came the rather curt answer.

'Hello, Thorri. This is Helgi Reykdal.'

'Helgi, nice to hear from you.' Immediately, Thorri's voice acquired a friendly, if insincere, note.

'Could we have a very quick chat, if you have a free moment? I expect you've got a lot on.'

'I certainly have. But I'm in the centre of town at the moment and free for the next hour, if that's any good. I don't know whether I can add anything to what I told you the other day, but we can meet up if you think it'll help.'

'That would be great.'

They agreed on a café, and Helgi headed over there. Despite having doubts about the decision he'd just taken – or rather that had been taken for him – he felt suddenly revitalized as he drove to the café. Writing his dissertation clearly hadn't been stimulating enough, but now he had what you might call a proper assignment, he felt far more cheerful than he had earlier that morning, as if he'd just been given an injection of energy.

Helgi couldn't immediately see the doctor as the café was crowded and Thorri turned out to be sitting in the corner by the entrance, absorbed in his laptop, under an old chandelier – or a chandelier that was designed to give the impression of being old. There was a buzz of activity in the place as it was gearing up for lunchtime, and no one paid Helgi any particular attention. He noticed that Thorri had a beer on the table in front of him. Deciding to stick to coffee himself, he went over to the counter to place his order.

He resisted the temptation to go for one of the array of delicious-looking cakes and pastries, though he had to drag his gaze away from a thick slab of chocolate cake. The woman serving behind the counter offered to bring his coffee over when it was ready, so he headed to where Thorri was sitting and greeted him.

Thorri looked up: 'Helgi, good to see you. Ground to a halt on your dissertation, have you?' He grinned and sipped his beer.

Helgi took a chair facing him.

'No, the dissertation is going fine. It was Tinna I wanted to talk to you about.'

'Yes, I saw the news this morning,' Thorri said. 'The poor woman. It's unbelievable. I mean, I can't claim to have known her well, but it's still a strange feeling to be acquainted with a murder victim.'

'Yes. And not for the first time either,' Helgi remarked.

'What?' It seemed to take Thorri a moment to catch on. 'Oh, I see what you mean. In Akureyri. Of course.'

'As a matter of fact,' Helgi said, his tone becoming serious, 'I've had to put my studies on hold as I've agreed to accept a position with Reykjavík CID, somewhat earlier than originally planned.'

Thorri appeared wrong-footed by this news.

'Oh? But you said you wanted to talk to me . . . about Tinna . . .'

'That's right. I was going to start work there in the summer or autumn, but Tinna's death has put the matter in a whole different light. I've been asked to take part in the investigation.'

'So, this means – what? – that I'm in the middle of a police interrogation here?' Thorri asked, and it wasn't clear whether he was being sarcastic or he was genuinely unhappy about this development. It wouldn't have surprised Helgi if he'd got up and walked out.

But Thorri didn't stir from his seat, for the moment at least.

'You could put it like that, I suppose,' Helgi replied, after a brief pause. 'In a sense. Would you have any objection to my asking you a few questions?'

'Do I have any choice?' Again, the question seemed to teeter between sarcasm and anger.

'When did you last see Tinna?'

'A long time ago, a very long time. It must have been at some kind of social event four or five years ago. To be honest, I can't remember exactly.'

'You didn't have any contact in the intervening years? You didn't, for example, discuss the deaths at the sanatorium with her at any point after she'd moved to Reykjavík?'

'Certainly not. And I can't imagine why you think I should have. If she'd wanted to talk to someone about that, she wouldn't exactly have had to look far, given that she was married to the detective who investigated the case.'

'Were you still director of the sanatorium when she left her job?'

'Yes, I was,' Thorri replied curtly.

'And was her decision to leave amicable?'

'Yes, I think I can safely say that. Of course, we were sorry to lose a good member of staff, but I knew it would be easy enough to find a replacement. Tinna was very competent at her job, but hardly indispensable. Still a bit wet behind the ears, if you know what I mean. So it wasn't a problem, everything was fine. Not like with Broddi.' He smiled and emptied his glass down his throat.

At that point the waitress brought Helgi's coffee to the table and Thorri seized the chance to order another beer.

'Did you have problems with Broddi, then?' Helgi asked.

'Well, obviously I had to let him go. Of course, that sort of thing is never easy. I almost felt sorry for the guy. He whined and protested like a little kid, then started blaming Ásta for the whole thing; kept going on about how it was all her fault. There were times when I thought he wasn't right in the head.'

'Sorry, who did you say he blamed for what?'

'Ásta. I can't remember the ins and outs of it, but I got the impression that he was blaming her for his dismissal. Which is crazy, given that she was long dead by then.'

'Who was this Ásta?'

'She worked at the sanatorium for many years as a nurse. I never met her, but Fridjón often spoke of her. She was an outstanding member of staff, apparently. A good, kind woman. That's why I'm inclined to think that Broddi must have had a screw loose – blaming his dismissal on a dead woman like that. The fact is, his work wasn't up to scratch, and, to make matters worse, he'd been arrested on suspicion of murder. Knowing that, I found his presence at the hospital uncomfortable.'

'Even though he was let off, an innocent man, and the investigating officers came to a different conclusion?' Helgi was disgusted by Thorri's heartless attitude and wondered how on earth he could have worked as a doctor all these years. In Helgi's opinion, doctors were supposed to be kind, sympathetic, understanding individuals . . . but none of these adjectives could be applied to the man in front of him.

'Well, it so happens that the violence stopped after Fridjón died,' Thorri said, 'so people were ready to swallow the theory that he was the killer. It was devastating for Fridjón's family, of course – his brother was still alive at the time. But extremely convenient for everyone else.'

'The killings stopped after Fridjón died, you say?'

'Right.' Thorri smiled.

'Until now.'

'Oh, well, yes, I suppose you could say that. But you don't seriously think the two cases are linked?'

'That's just what I've been asked to find out.'

'I have to say, I find the idea absurd,' Thorri retorted sharply.

'Where were you the night Tinna died – the night before last, that is?'

'Are you joking?' The doctor's voice rose in outrage.

'We need to know.'

'Surely the most likely scenario is that her husband – the policeman – did it? A domestic crime, in other words. It's hardly unheard of. Domestic violence is becoming more of a problem all the time.'

Helgi tried to ignore the way his stomach twisted at these words. He had to stay professional.

'You can rest assured that the possibility will be taken into consideration,' he answered formally. 'Anyway, where were you at the time?'

'Where do you think? I was at home, of course, asleep in bed. That is, I've got a house in Gardabær, as well as the one in Akureyri.'

'Were you alone?'

'Yes, I usually am when I'm in Reykjavík. My wife works in Akureyri and rarely comes south with me.'

'Were you at home all night?'

'Of course.'

Helgi nodded. The business about Broddi blaming a woman called Ásta was worth exploring further, he reflected, but apart from that he hadn't learnt much of interest from the conversation. As for Thorri's claim that he had been alone at home when the murder happened, it wouldn't have taken him more than about fifteen minutes to drive from Gardabær to Árbær at night if he'd wanted to kill Tinna.

There was one more point Helgi meant to raise with the doctor: 'While I remember, what sort of relationship did you have with Elísabet?'

Thorri glanced up, frowning: 'What are you implying?'

'I gather you two were close at one time.'

'Who the hell said that? It's complete bullshit.'

'So there's nothing to it?'

Thorri hesitated. 'There was never anything going on between us,' he said emphatically. 'But I won't deny that she may have had her hopes that things would work out differently. There was a while when she simply wouldn't leave me alone. She wanted us to get together and said she was going to leave her husband . . . It was embarrassing, to be honest.'

'And you did nothing to encourage it?'

'Nothing at all. The attraction was completely one-sided and the situation became increasingly uncomfortable. It was a welcome relief when I was offered the position of director at the County Hospital.'

'But everything's fine between you now?'

Thorri smiled coldly: 'I have absolutely no contact with the woman. I doubt I'd even recognize her if I saw her in the street.'

2012

Helgi

Elísabet turned out to live in a smallish flat in one of the modern blocks on Sóltún.

She had readily invited Helgi round when he rang her, though she said she wouldn't be free until six o'clock. He suspected this was a subterfuge to make it look as though she was busier than she really was. He had been hoping to see Broddi too, but he hadn't managed to get hold of him until that afternoon, so he had arranged to meet him the following day.

Elísabet's furniture was modern and rather tasteless; the kind of stuff that wouldn't stand much wear and tear. Helgi got the impression that she hadn't taken anything with her from her old life with her late husband when she moved south in search of a fresh start but had spent money on new furnishings that she could ill afford. The sitting room had a large French window with a Venetian blind, a newish-looking tube television of a type Helgi hadn't thought was being manufactured any more, a scarlet sofa and a black coffee table that appeared to be made of plastic rather than wood. Apart from this, the sitting room was sparsely furnished. There wasn't even a dining table, though there would have been room for one, and there were no paintings on the walls, just a few framed family photos on top of the TV set.

Elísabet had made coffee and now offered Helgi a tin of gingerbread biscuits.

'Thanks for inviting me round. Nice flat you've got here,' he said politely. They were both sitting on the sofa, with as much distance between them as possible.

'Thank you. I'm quite pleased with it. Of course, it's a bit different from the house I lived in up north, but it's also a lot less work.' She smiled, but her smile was melancholy.

'I think it's only right to begin by informing you that I'm now working for the police,' Helgi said.

The news had quite an effect on her.

'For the police? What do you mean?'

'I used to work for them before I left to pursue my studies, and now I've taken over a new role. It all happened a little sooner than planned because of Tinna's death, which I've agreed to investigate.'

'Oh, well . . .' Elísabet's chest rose and fell, and he noticed that her hands were trembling a little. 'I just don't understand what you want from me . . .'

Helgi smiled in an attempt to lighten the atmosphere and said in a friendly voice: 'I'm simply trying to find out whether there could be any hidden links between this incident and the old case in Akureyri.'

'Good grief, no! Is that what you think? No, there can't be. That's impossible.'

'It is a bit of a long shot, I agree, but my boss – his name's Magnús – wanted me to run the idea past you and your former colleagues. I can assure you that the main focus of the investigation is elsewhere, however.'

'Elsewhere? On Sverrir, you mean? I never liked him.' She snorted. Her hands were no longer trembling.

'I can't discuss that, I'm afraid, but I wanted a quick chat with you, in the light of this latest development.' He took a sip of what turned out to be lukewarm coffee, but then he had arrived ten minutes late. 'Good coffee,' he said.

'Thanks. It's only filter, but I should know how to make it at my age.'

'Can you think of anything at all that might help clarify what's happened? Anything from the past? I repeat that I find it pretty unlikely that there could be any connection.'

'I . . . er, no, I can't think of anything off the top of my head. To be honest, I'm still recovering from the shock of hearing that Tinna's dead. Do they suspect her Sverrir?'

'I'm afraid I have no information about that. My colleagues are investigating that side of things. You didn't run into her at all after we last spoke?'

'No, I didn't. Why would you think that?'

'I was only asking. Incidentally, have you been here in town all week?'

'Yes, of course. Why?'

'I've been asked to check whether any of you had met her – gone round to her house, for example . . .'

'Any of us?'

'Yes, I mean you, Broddi or Thorri.'

'Have you spoken to Thorri?' she asked immediately.

'I met him at lunchtime, yes.'

She was silent for a moment, then said: 'No, I haven't seen her. Why should I have done?'

'It happened the night before last, as you're probably aware.'

Elísabet nodded.

'Were you at home then?' Helgi knew he shouldn't put words in the mouths of the people he was questioning, but he judged that this approach would be less likely to spook Elísabet.

'Yes, yes, of course, I was at home. You can't think . . .'

'No, no, don't worry,' Helgi assured her. Then added: 'I assume you were alone?'

'Yes, I was alone. I've been alone ever since my husband died. My son's abroad and I don't have many other people to turn to,' she said plaintively. Then she repeated: 'But surely you don't think that I . . . that . . . I mean, I wouldn't hurt a fly.'

Elísabet was quite strongly built, despite being in her sixties. No doubt she had been even stronger in her youth. Helgi could imagine her being physically capable of carrying out Yrsa's murder. And Tinna had apparently been suffocated with a pillow. Although the signs were that she had put up a fight, no biological traces had been found from her killer, according to the email Magnús had sent Helgi filling him in on the main facts of the case.

'Do you remember a woman called Ásta who used to

work at the sanatorium?' Helgi asked, judging that this was a good moment to change the subject.

'Ásta? Yes, I know who she was. Why do you ask?'

'Did you know her?'

'No, I wouldn't say that. She'd left by the time I started, but she used to drop by every now and then to visit her old colleagues. She must have died in around 1975, and would have been quite old by then. I started working there in 1970, so I often encountered her.'

'What kind of person was she?'

'Lovely. She literally radiated warmth. Everyone spoke well of her, and I remember what nice things the vicar said about her in his funeral address. She'd worked as a nurse all her life and had seen some big changes in her time. TB was still rife when she started at the sanatorium. It must have been terrible in those days.'

Helgi nodded.

'But why are you asking about her?'

Helgi paused to consider before answering, unsure how much he ought to share with this woman.

'Her name came up in conversation. I just wanted to know a bit more about her, like whether she could have been linked to the deaths in some way, directly or indirectly.'

'No, are you crazy? The poor woman was long dead by 1983.'

She offered him the tin of gingerbread again.

'Do have one. I know Christmas was ages ago, but you can never have too much gingerbread.'

'Thanks.' He took one.

'What kind of cases will you be handling in the police?' she asked conversationally. 'Won't it be hard for you to finish your studies if you're working?' She smiled and took a sip of coffee, and Helgi could sense her desperation to prolong his visit.

He ended up sitting with Elísabet for more than an hour. She gave off such an oppressive aura of loneliness, of longing for company, that he hadn't liked to leave immediately. She'd asked him all about himself, and he had actually found himself telling her about Bergthóra and their debate over whether to continue renting or to buy a flat.

In spite of this, he got home in time for a late supper with Bergthóra, their regular weekly casserole.

'So, I start tomorrow morning,' he announced. He hadn't rung her with the news, preferring to break it to her in person, face to face, to see if he'd actually succeed in making her happy.

'Start?'

'With the police.'

'Wow, about time,' she said warmly. 'Congratulations, darling.'

'As a matter of fact, I've started already. But tomorrow's my official first day.'

'Are they giving you something interesting to work on?'

'Yes, I'm investigating the murder in Árbær.'

'Seriously?' Bergthóra's eyebrows lifted at this.

'Yes, you remember, I told you that the woman who was murdered had a connection to my dissertation; she used to work at the sanatorium.'

'What a coincidence. And a great way to get involved in the case,' she said. 'Shall we open a bottle of wine to celebrate?'

'I . . . I'm afraid I need to work,' he said awkwardly, which was true, but the fact was he didn't like the idea of drinking.

'You could at least spend a bit of time with me first.' Her voice rose on an aggrieved note. 'I'm shattered after the day I've had and could do with relaxing.'

'Well, we'll see. If I have time.'

'Right, fine. Do what you like. I'm going to have a glass, anyway.'

Helgi had been in no mood to share a bottle of red with Bergthóra. It would only end in a fight, as so often before. She'd gone ahead and opened the wine while he took refuge in the study with the old case notes. He wanted to reread them carefully, in case he had overlooked something.

He'd felt the pull of the detective novels as he passed the shelves in the sitting room, but they would have to wait. There were more books in the study that he'd like to have immersed himself in – an overspill from the other room, mostly foreign whodunnits. He brushed his fingers over the spines: Agatha Christie, Ellery Queen, S. S. Van Dine, but this evening his attention was reserved for the old sanatorium.

It simply couldn't be a coincidence that Tinna had been murdered just when he had started probing people's memories of the case. There had to be a link.

Unless Thorri had been right: that the solution to the mystery lay in domestic violence. If so, the police were bound to prise the truth out of Sverrir sooner or later. All Helgi could do was carry on delving into the past.

As the evening wore on and the words began to blur in front of his eyes, he switched to studying old photos of the scene. It was hard to look at the ones of Yrsa, given the abhorrent nature of the attack – the pool of blood on the desk, the amputated fingers. The woman had so obviously been subjected to torture before being killed. Nevertheless, he forced himself to pore over each picture until finally one of them gave him pause. It was a photo of the objects in her desk drawers, taken as a matter of course in order to create a detailed record of the scene. The drawers contained documents, keys, memos and notes, all more or less illegible, but under one file there was a glimpse of a photo, an old black-and-white snapshot of a little boy. Although only half of his face was visible, it caught Helgi's attention. Had she had a son? He couldn't remember reading anything about that in the case notes, but if she had, it would certainly be worth talking to him.

2012

Helgi

Helgi arrived at the police station the following morning at 10.15, as arranged. He was going to meet Broddi after lunch. This appeared to him to be the most obvious next step in the investigation, though he wanted to talk to Sverrir too. And his thoughts kept returning to that black-and-white photo of the little boy. He had to find out whether Yrsa had had a son who might still be alive.

'Good to see you, Helgi, my boy,' Magnús greeted him with cheerful familiarity. 'First day on the job, eh? We'll start calculating your wages as of now.'

'Fantastic.'

'Have you started looking into the Tinna business at all?'

'Yes, as a matter of fact I spoke to two of her former colleagues yesterday – people who used to work with her at the sanatorium in Akureyri. I'm meeting the third later today, so I should be able to put something together for you very soon. Incidentally, it would be great if I could talk to Sverrir as well. Would that be OK?'

'Yes, but let's just hang on with that. We've got him in the cells at the moment, but he's here of his own free will. We didn't want to go to the lengths of requesting a custody order. Obviously, it's a delicate matter since he's a former police officer and we don't have any solid evidence against him. There's nothing to incriminate him in the murder apart from the fact he was married to Tinna and doesn't have a watertight alibi. Still, I'll see if you can have a chat with him this evening or tomorrow morning.

'By the way, there's a slight hitch with your office,' Magnús went on smoothly. 'The woman who's leaving us, she – ah – she hasn't quite gone yet. She'll be here for a few more days to wrap up her cases, so I was wondering if you wouldn't mind working from home in the meantime? I'll try to get her out of the way as soon as possible.'

'Yes, sure, that's fine. I'm not in any hurry.'

'Do have a look at the office anyway. I gather she's gone out somewhere.'

Magnús got to his feet and showed Helgi to the door of the office in question, where he left him with a firm shake of the hand: 'Welcome to the team, Helgi. It's great to have you on board.'

'Thanks.'

Once Magnús had gone, Helgi put his head round the door of the office. It was indeed empty, though obviously still very much in use as there were piles of paperwork everywhere. He slipped inside, feeling as if he were trespassing on someone else's property. The office was reasonably spacious and he could picture himself being happy there. Behind the desk was a bookcase that was only partially filled. He might be able to keep some of his old novels in it. That would make the place feel a bit more homely. The chair looked pretty comfortable, if a bit battered. He stood by the desk for a while, breathing in the atmosphere. This is where he would be working for the next few years at least.

He felt an urge to try out the chair and get a feel for his workspace, so, after a moment's hesitation, he sat down, hoping that the woman, who still had to clear her office, wouldn't choose that moment to return.

As he sat there, his eye fell on a sheet of paper, on which some familiar names were written. Evidently, she had been looking into Tinna's case. There were three names: Tinna, Broddi and Thorri, and some scribbled notes dotted with question marks, but the only thing Helgi could make out was: '*Previous job??*' The comment referred, as far as he could tell, to Thorri.

Previous job? Did this mean at the sanatorium? Or prior to that?

Where did Thorri say he'd worked . . . ?

At Hvammstangi, that was it. Helgi recalled the man's strange hesitation before answering the perfectly harmless question.

Maybe it would be worth taking a look into how his job there had ended.

2012

Helgi

Helgi bounded up the stairs of the block of flats where Broddi lived, all the way to the third floor, for the second time in just over a week. He'd explained on the phone that there had been a change in his circumstances, but Broddi hadn't sounded remotely perturbed by this news. 'Once a cop, always a cop,' was his only comment.

His flat was as small and airless as Helgi had remembered. He hadn't felt particularly comfortable there on his previous visit, but he'd put up with it then and could do so now.

They sat at the kitchen table, and Broddi offered him the inevitable coffee and Danish pastry.

'I wasn't expecting to see you again so soon, Helgi, but it's always nice to have visitors. You didn't mention it on the phone, but I assume you want to talk about Tinna.'

'That's right.'

'I suppose you want to know where I was when she

was murdered. I understand from the news that it happened in the middle of the night.'

Helgi nodded.

'As I'm sure you'll have guessed, I can't give you an alibi to prove I didn't do it. Because I'm always here at home, see, every night the same, never any change, alone with my memories. All I can say is that I had nothing to do with it. You'll just have to take my word for that. I was fond of Tinna, and the only explanation I can think of is that it must have been a family tragedy. I'd believe anything of that bastard Sverrir. He had me locked up and tried to pin a murder on me, as you know. When I looked him in the eye, I could tell he wasn't a good man. So I wouldn't be the slightest bit surprised to hear that he was violent too.' He sighed heavily. 'Poor Tinna.'

Helgi hadn't been prepared for a denunciation like this, but he reminded himself that Broddi's opinion of Sverrir would have to be taken with a pinch of salt. The old caretaker wasn't exactly an impartial witness.

He wanted to believe Broddi, sensing that the man had suffered enough over the years, but of course he couldn't rule him out. Even at his age he wouldn't have had much trouble suffocating Tinna. He still looked pretty robust.

'Tell me, Broddi, did Yrsa have any children?'

'Well, that's one question I can answer,' Broddi said. 'She definitely didn't have any children.'

'Are you quite sure?'

'As sure as can be. She never went near a man, never started a family. What makes you think she had kids?'

'There was a photo of a little boy among her belongings.'

'A little boy?' Broddi sounded surprised. 'Can I see it?'

'I'm afraid I don't have a copy on me,' Helgi said.

'Well, it would be interesting to see it,' Broddi said, sounding as if he meant it. 'But Yrsa never had any children of her own, I'm sure of that.'

'Who's Ásta?' Helgi asked, curious to see Broddi's reaction.

Although the man's expression was hard to read, Helgi thought he looked a little disconcerted.

'Ásta? I don't know any Ásta,' Broddi answered shortly.

'Are you absolutely sure?'

Broddi thought for a moment, then answered: 'Positive. Who is this Ásta?'

'She used to work at the sanatorium.'

'Oh, *her*, yes, I remember her all right. Why on earth are you asking about her?'

'So you did know Ásta?' Helgi said, fairly confident that Broddi had been playing for time.

'Yes, I knew her, of course, but it just didn't occur to me that you were talking about that Ásta. I haven't thought about her for donkey's years. Anyway, she was long dead by the time Yrsa and Fridjón died, so she can't have had anything to do with that business.' A note of irritation had entered his voice.

'Oh, I understood that you kept bringing her name up,' Helgi said, without elaborating.

'That I kept bringing her name up?' Broddi laughed. 'That's crazy. I mean, yes, we overlapped at the sanatorium for several years – I don't remember exactly how many. And after she retired she used to show her face from time to time, turning up with home-made cakes and doughnuts, probably trying to distract herself from her loneliness.' He was silent for a moment, then added: 'As we all do.'

'So you didn't have any other contact with her after she left?'

'Definitely not,' Broddi said firmly, and this time Helgi believed him, the conviction in his voice was so strong. Broddi leaned forward across the table, his eyes narrowed: 'Who said I did?'

'It doesn't matter.'

'It does matter,' Broddi said. 'Because it's happened before, Helgi. It's all happened before, can't you see?'

And then Helgi realized what the old caretaker was implying.

'They've tried to pin the blame on me before, the whole lot of them, maybe individually, maybe in cahoots, what do I know? . . . But the reason is always the same. I was just a humble caretaker, so it was fine to sacrifice me, fine to throw me to the lions.'

2012

Helgi

Helgi's heart missed a beat when he saw the bottles on the table – two empty red wine bottles. And a half-full glass on a bookshelf, right next to his precious detective novels. Bergthóra was nowhere to be seen; probably – hopefully – gone to bed. He removed the glass from the shelf and took it through to the kitchen, treading softly so as not to wake Bergthóra if she was asleep. There was a deathly hush in the flat. It was so quiet that in a flash of fear he thought something might have happened.

The silence was almost oppressive, but he wasn't going to let it get to him. He was hit by a weary longing to sleep on the sofa again, to calm himself down with a book and leave Bergthóra to sleep it off without giving her the gratification of checking up on her.

He stood there irresolutely for a while, listening to the silence and wondering which old whodunnit he should take down from the shelves, which book would help restore his emotional equilibrium and calm his nerves. The lighting in the sitting room was cosily dim, only the floor lamp was on, but it had been enough to reveal the bottles and the glass.

He smelt the faint, dry smell of old books, saw a tempting vision of the sofa and himself lying there, his fatigue easing off as he deliberately turned his thoughts away from Bergthóra.

He lost his balance with such shocking suddenness that it took him a second to realize what was happening. A violent shove had sent him toppling forwards to land face first against the bookcase.

After a few stunned moments, he whipped round, his face stinging from the impact, and managed to ward off the next attack. She lunged at him with her bare fists, but he got his arm across his face first in an instinct for self-preservation.

He closed his eyes briefly – an automatic reaction – then, opening them, did his best to dodge her blows. He never responded with force, never took advantage of his superior physical strength or laid a hand on Bergthóra; it had never even crossed his mind to react any other way. He just wasn't the type. He fended off her onslaught for a while, hoping it would pass, accepting the pain that spread through his body.

This time, however, Bergthóra seemed to be possessed of an unheard-of strength, determined to keep going to the bitter end. He lowered his arm slightly from his face and met her raging gaze. 'Darling, what are you doing? Why are you hitting me?'

'You've been horrible to me, Helgi. Horrible. You have no right to treat me like that.'

Her voice rose in pitch with every word. 'You always seem happy when you're with other people . . . Perhaps it's just me you can't stand? Is that it?'

'Don't be silly, Bergthóra. You've had too much to drink.' *Way too much*, he wanted to add, but he knew it would only make matters worse. In this situation it was best to say as little as possible and avoid shifting the blame from him on to her. She never came up with any rational reasons for her violence. By the time she was on her second bottle the most trivial source of friction between them would escalate into a major row. She would find fault with everything he did, all her insecurities bursting forth in a blind fury. He never felt an answering anger these days, only pity. And he was never genuinely afraid, although a couple of times she had come close to seriously injuring him. He simply tried to remain calm, as this was usually the only thing that worked, the only way to pacify her. The first few times she'd raised a hand to him he had lost his temper and yelled at her, threatening her in return, but that had been like pouring oil on the flames. His initial impulse had been to leave her, but then he'd tried to understand – the underlying causes rather than the actions themselves. Tried to work out what had made his girlfriend like this.

She lifted her hand to strike him again, but this time he successfully dodged out of range.

'That's right, run away, Helgi, you pathetic shit,' she slurred. Again and again he had resorted to disposing of all the alcohol in the house, but this only ever won him a temporary respite. Bergthóra knew all the tricks in the book; a regular customer in the state off-licences, she was forever stashing away bottles, so the truth was that he was never safe. And when the shops were shut, there was nothing to stop her walking into a bar, only to come home later burning with resentment at the world.

Sometimes he thought they'd got over it. Those were the times when they had gone several weeks without a drink; when all was quiet and Bergthóra seemed in better spirits, hovering on the edge of a smile. Then back they would lurch into the same deadly cycle. Sometimes he thought he detected warning signs, black clouds forming over her head, but for the most part the storm would strike totally out of the blue.

They had discussed seeking outside help more than once. Helgi spoke of couples' counselling, though of course he knew that the causes ran deeper. In these conversations they skirted around Bergthóra's alcohol problem and her traumatic childhood experiences, though she had opened up about them in the past. Then there was the violence. Of course, it was a police matter, but it had never occurred to Helgi to go down that route. These were the real problems they had to solve, so any talk of relationship counselling was pure window-dressing. Not that Bergthóra would even agree to that, merely insisting that she was dealing with her issues. How, he didn't know. But he himself had recently taken a step closer to sorting out his future, though he'd done it alone, without support. He'd booked an appointment with a therapist for himself, behind

Bergthóra's back. Gradually it had dawned on him that *he* needed to talk to someone, that being the victim in this relationship was harder to bear than he'd acknowledged to himself. Men weren't supposed to cry, but sometimes the need to break down in tears was almost more than he could bear.

They both stood motionless, not saying a word. She stared at him, her eyes blazing with fury and hate. This wasn't the woman he loved – or used to love. Alcohol had turned her into a stranger.

'I'm going out, love,' he said, heading for the hall. 'I'll be back later, once you've calmed down.'

He turned his back on her, half expecting her to strike him or shove him or worse, but he wasn't going to give her the satisfaction of looking round.

Then he heard a succession of thuds and spun round to see her snatching books from the shelves – his precious books, his father's classic collection. She was hurling them on the floor with such violence that he had never seen anything like it. In an instant the floor was covered in books and, before he could react, she had grabbed another, an old paperback, and started ripping the pages out of it.

'Your fucking books!' she screamed. 'You love them more than me. You've always loved . . .'

He snatched the paperback away from her and put it back on the shelf. 'What the fuck are you doing, Bergthóra?'

She swept more books on to the floor and trampled on them, then pushed Helgi so hard he almost fell over.

Recovering his balance, he positioned himself in front of the bookcase. 'Go to the bedroom right now and lie down, or *I'll* be the one ringing the police.'

'Do as you like,' she retorted. 'I'll tell them you attacked me.'

This was a new threat. The strength of her vindictiveness seemed to grow every time she got into this state.

'Tell them what?' He was shaken.

'That *you* attacked *me*!'

Helgi took a step towards her and put his arms warily around her shoulders. He could feel her untensing a little.

'Bergthóra, you've got to calm down. You need to rest. I don't know what I've done to upset you, but you've had too much to drink, love.'

'I had a few glasses,' she said, in a quieter voice.

He looked at the books littering the floor and the torn paperback on the shelf. His only copy of *Peril at End House*, one of the first translations of Agatha Christie into Icelandic, a book that his father had cherished. Helgi felt hurt and distressed by the wanton destruction, but he tried not to be angry. He drew a deep breath. It was only a book, after all, even if it was irreplaceable.

He wasn't going to lose his temper, because that was exactly what she wanted; to provoke him to anger, to elicit a reaction. There was nothing to be gained from that. He had to de-escalate the situation, as he had been taught at police training college, so he tried to view Bergthóra's behaviour as just another conflict to be managed, as if she were a stranger who had nothing to do with him.

When he led her into the bedroom, she didn't try to resist. Perhaps she was tired, or had done enough damage for the time being. As he helped her into bed, she let out a whimper, then a gasp and another gasp, her shoulders shaking uncontrollably. He took her in his arms and, as so often happened, her anger dissolved in a storm of weeping and she lay sobbing in his embrace like a weary child, while his heart turned over inside him. At long last her sobs quietened and he realized she was asleep. Gently detaching himself, he got up off the bed and stood there for a while, watching her and thinking.

Luckily, her flare-up had been over fairly quickly this time, so he hoped there wouldn't be any visits from the neighbour or the police. But, as always, it was Helgi who was left to deal with the problem. He felt an even greater determination to attend his appointment with the therapist, although it was Bergthóra who needed therapy. And he asked himself whether this was the final straw. Whether it wasn't time to break free of this vicious cycle once and for all by the simple expedient of walking out on her.

2012

Helgi

Bergthóra was still asleep when Helgi crept out of the house at ten the following morning. This time he remembered to take the photo from the scene of Yrsa's murder with him, as somehow he needed to find out the identity of the boy in the old black-and-white snapshot.

Helgi had rung Bergthóra's office to report that she was ill. These episodes tended to happen at weekends, as that way she knew she could hide the fall-out from her drinking, but occasionally her problem spilled over into the week, leading to dark days like this one.

He was at his wits' end. Her attacks of violent rage seemed to be intensifying, she wouldn't hear of seeking help and he kept having to cover up for her. Naturally, the neighbour upstairs was convinced that Helgi was the aggressor and Bergthóra his victim, and he guessed that his colleagues from the police, who had recently paid them a visit, suspected the same. It wouldn't enter anyone's head that it could be the other way round.

It was just as well that he had an appointment with the therapist later that day, but first on the agenda was a trip to the Directorate of Health, whose offices were located in a grand old building near the indoor swimming pool. He had arranged to meet a woman who had promised to find out what she could about Thorri's career. Being in the police certainly opened doors, as he was discovering.

He was shown up the impressive spiral staircase to the top floor, where a woman of around his own age was waiting on the landing. She was petite, with short dark hair. 'You must be Helgi,' she greeted him with a smile.

'That's right.'

'Nice to meet you. My name's Aníta. Do come in.' She showed him into a small office and took a seat behind the computer screen on the desk.

'It's not every day I get a request from CID,' she said archly. 'I'm sure it's of grave importance, but I have to admit that I'm enjoying the novelty.'

'I'm glad to hear it,' he replied, appreciating the way this young woman didn't seem to take life too seriously. He'd woken up this morning with his nerves in tatters following Bergthóra's episode yesterday evening, so Aníta's cheeriness came as a welcome relief. 'Though I assume you realize that we've got to guard this secret with our lives. The doctor in question mustn't find out that I've been asking questions about him. You can't breathe a word about this to anyone else.'

'Of course.' She looked at the screen. 'Actually, this is a bit odd, Helgi.'

'Odd?'

'Yes. You asked me to find out why he left his job in Hvammstangi, didn't you?'

'Yes, that's right.'

'The trouble is, he never worked in Hvammstangi.'

'I'm sorry? Are you sure about that?'

'Quite sure.' She smiled.

'Well I never.'

'Does that mean he lied to you?'

Helgi chose not to answer this but asked instead: 'Was the job at the sanatorium his first position, then?'

'No, he'd worked in Húsavík previously.'

'How strange.'

'Yes, it's hard to mix up Hvammstangi and Húsavík, especially if you worked in one place and not the other,' Aníta said, with a humorous lift of her eyebrow.

'Why did he leave?' Helgi asked.

'That's odd too,' she said with a grin, evidently enjoying this.

'Go on.'

'He was on a three-year contract, and I can assure you that junior doctors almost invariably see their contracts through. That's how the system works. People are entrusted with a job and, once it's finished, they apply for a new contract or a placement somewhere else. All within fixed parameters. But our friend Thorri left after barely two years. Then he was unemployed for six months or so until he got the position in Akureyri. I even came across some old reports by his boss in Húsavík relating to the termination of his employment. He wrote that he and Thorri had come to a mutual understanding that he would leave on the grounds that he wasn't suited to the job.'

'Do you happen to have his boss's name?' Helgi asked, hoping against hope that the man was still alive.

'Yes, he's well known – a respected name in the profession. Getting on for ninety now, but still going strong. You'll want to talk to him, won't you?'

'It might be interesting.'

'His name's Matthías. Matthías Ólafsson. You'll find him in the telephone directory.'

2012

Helgi

'Tell me more about your girlfriend, Helgi.'

The therapist seemed relaxed but attentive.

This was Helgi's second visit. The first had been restricted to a general conversation, no doubt a deliberate policy by the therapist to put him at his ease, but now they were finally getting to the heart of the matter. Helgi hadn't asked anyone for recommendations but found the man himself online. He just needed to talk to someone – preferably a stranger – he could trust.

'We've been together a long time. The violence didn't begin straight away, well, not quite, but fairly early on. And it's been getting steadily worse.'

'I see.' The therapist nodded. 'Does it tend to happen in a particular set of circumstances?'

'It's usually triggered by alcohol, which seems to bring out her aggression.' Helgi's throat felt tight. He'd never been forced to put this into words before and was finding it harder than he had imagined possible.

'Has she received treatment for her drinking?'

'She would never hear of it. Alcohol's not the problem, not in itself. It's the violence that's the problem.'

Again, the therapist nodded. 'I see. We don't need to worry about exact definitions at this stage. Let's try instead to get to the root of the problem.'

'OK,' Helgi agreed meekly.

'Tell me, Helgi, what form does the violence take?'

Although Helgi had been expecting the question, part of him had hoped not to be asked.

'It varies. Sometimes she just lashes out at me, at others she really goes for me, beating me as hard as she can. I try to defend myself, of course, but I never hit back – it wouldn't occur to me to do that. I'm never scared – not genuinely frightened, you know – but obviously I'm not happy about it. We're always having noisy rows, and it's just not normal. Sometimes she goes further and resorts to weapons. I suppose that's when I'm most worried about getting injured, though luckily I've got off lightly so far, but a lot of stuff gets broken in the process. And sometimes she tries to harm herself.'

'In what way?' the therapist asked in a calm, level voice, as if this were merely an academic question.

'The other day she grabbed a knife from the kitchen,' Helgi replied, heaving a deep breath. This was so hard for him to admit. He'd never wanted to discuss the problem, but now that he was doing so, he realized it helped to unburden himself to somebody, even if it never led to anything. 'At first she aimed it at me – the knife, I mean – but at no point was I afraid she was serious. I got the impression she was just attention-seeking. Then she cut herself and drew blood, though luckily it wasn't deep. I had to take the knife away from her by force.'

'How did the fight end?'

'Oh, our upstairs neighbour rang the police. It took all my powers of persuasion to get rid of the officers who came round, but I managed, thank God. They would almost certainly have misinterpreted the situation and arrested me, though I've never laid a finger on Bergthóra. After they'd gone, I saw that there was blood on my shirt, but luckily they didn't notice.' Having got this off his chest, Helgi let out a long breath.

'How do you feel, Helgi, after she has acted like this – used violence against you, I mean?'

Helgi considered this. Once again, he'd been caught unprepared, not having expected to have to find words to express what went through his mind at those times.

'I still care about her,' he said eventually, groping for the right words. 'Still love her, in spite of everything. I think. We've always had this . . . well, this strong physical attraction, and usually that's been enough to help us overcome any dramas or differences between us. And sometimes it still is. Of course, her behaviour's totally unacceptable, I'm well aware of that, and maybe I ought to be a bit tougher in response, but I don't know what good that would do. All I do know is that something has to change, but I've no idea how to make it happen. Perhaps that's why I've come to you, to get help with that.'

'Why aren't you tougher in response, Helgi?'

This time he really had to stop and think about his answer. He had decided to see a therapist in the hope it would make him feel a little better about the situation, but now he had to make a decision. Was he going to bring up the subject or not? Should he trust the expert?

'In a way it's not her fault,' he said, then immediately regretted the way he'd phrased it. Of course she was responsible for her own behaviour, but what he meant was that the blame for the underlying causes lay elsewhere, to a degree.

'What do you mean by that, Helgi?' the therapist asked in an unsettlingly hypnotic voice that made Helgi feel compelled to answer.

'It's not something we – Bergthóra and I – really talk about these days.' The words seemed to stick in his throat and he had to force them out. 'She experienced abuse at school.'

'Abuse? What kind of abuse?'

'Long-term mental abuse. From a teacher. It went on pretty much right through her time at school.'

'Ah, is that so?' the therapist said, his voice still level, clearly not easily disconcerted.

'The situation's got worse over the years – her depressive moods, her aggression – but it's clear that her problems can be traced back to that time.'

'Mental abuse, you say. Not physical?'

'Not in her case.' Helgi sighed. 'But her friend didn't get off so lightly.'

'Oh?'

'She was subjected to physical violence by the teacher in question, and worse too, from what I understand. She killed herself in her teens. She was Bergthóra's best friend.'

'I see,' the therapist said in an icy tone.

'And I'm pretty sure that Bergthóra's never got over it.'

2012

Helgi

Magnús rang just as Helgi was on his way to meet Thorri's one-time boss, the elderly doctor Matthías Ólafsson. It was getting on for seven o'clock and Helgi had eaten a burger from a fast-food place for supper, having no desire to see Bergthóra yet. He wanted to give her a chance to recover and reflect on her behaviour.

'Helgi, my boy, am I interrupting anything?' Magnús asked.

'No, you're fine, I'm just on my way to follow up a lead.'

'Good, good. You wanted to speak to Sverrir, didn't you?'

'Yes, very much.'

'Then drop by. He's still here, but I don't think we're going to hold him any longer. We don't have a shred of evidence against him.'

Damn. Helgi didn't want to break his appointment

with the old doctor. 'Would it be OK if I came in an hour?'

'Well, all right, I suppose we can hang on till then.'

Matthías received Helgi in the lounge of the retirement home where he lived. They took a seat on a fairly comfortable corner sofa, having accepted cake and coffee from the staff doing the evening trolley round.

'My children wanted me to move here,' Matthías said. 'They were worried about me. Though I think it's just because of my age, you know. I'll be ninety in three years' time and they don't believe I can look after myself any longer. But one shouldn't take age too literally.'

There was some truth in that, Helgi thought, since the man looked more like seventy than eighty-seven, with his handsome mane of thick grey hair, shrewd eyes and few obvious signs of physical deterioration. Matthías was formally dressed in a grey suit, a shirt and a red tie, as if he were about to go on duty.

'It's not often that I'm asked to talk to the police these days, though I used to have dealings with your colleagues from time to time when I was working, of course. Doctors get to see a thing or two, as you can imagine.'

'I can. Anyway, I hope I won't need to keep you long, Matthías. Thank you so much for taking the time to meet me.'

'Time? I've got nothing but time now. No one wants to employ a doctor in his eighties, so I spend my days reading and doing a bit of research.' He smiled. 'I've got all the time in the world, in one sense.'

'I wanted to ask you about a doctor who used to work for you many years ago. It's connected to an ongoing investigation, so I'll have to request that you keep it confidential.'

'Of course. I'm an expert in that area. Who was the doctor?'

'Thorri Thorsteinsson. Do you remember him?'

'Thorri, yes. Of course. We worked together in Húsavík. Not for very long, though. An excellent doctor, intelligent too, but – well, he had a problem.'

'What kind of problem was that?'

'Now you're asking. I haven't spoken about this to many people, Helgi, but I assume you must have a good reason for wanting to know . . .' Matthías left this hanging, somewhere between a statement and a question.

'It's safe to say that I do,' Helgi reassured him.

'I had to let him go, you see. He, well, he had a little problem, as I said – with drugs . . .'

'Drugs?'

'He kept turning up late or missing work, and in the end he admitted to me that he'd been experimenting with certain substances but that it had got out of hand and he had stopped. Some pills had gone missing from the hospital pharmacy and he confessed to having taken them. I had no choice but to let him go, though I took him at his word that he had quit and was intending to get himself back on the straight and narrow. He was young and quite promising, and I reckon everyone deserves a second chance. But I couldn't be the one to offer him that chance because he'd betrayed my trust. However, I omitted to mention this in the paperwork referring to his dismissal. I just hope he didn't go off the rails again, but I didn't believe he would.'

Drugs might not be an issue any more, Helgi thought, but, from what he had seen, Thorri was clearly fond of a drink.

'Were you aware that he had been taken on by the old sanatorium in Akureyri?'

'Of course. Fridjón got in touch. We knew each other quite well.'

'Did you tell him the truth?'

'I did, but strictly in confidence. As I said, it wouldn't have served any purpose to put obstacles in Thorri's way, but I couldn't lie to Fridjón. So I gave Thorri a good reference in other respects and said I hoped he'd turned a corner in relation to his drug problem. As a matter of fact, Thorri had applied to work on a research project there, specifically to avoid having any dealings with patients and medicines – to start with, anyway. If I remember right, he wanted to research the history of tuberculosis in the north of Iceland, including treatments and other aspects that involved digging around in the archives. I had no reservations about recommending him for that type of work.'

'Do you know if anything emerged from his research?'

'I don't, to be honest. Probably just some report that ended up lying unread in a drawer at the ministry. Who knows?'

'You say that Fridjón was well aware of Thorri's secret,' Helgi said thoughtfully, speaking more to himself than to

Matthías. 'Which the respected doctor presumably wouldn't have wanted to become common knowledge . . .'

'I see what you're thinking, Helgi,' Matthías said with a wry smile. 'You're wondering whether Thorri could have pushed poor old Fridjón off that balcony.'

'It did cross my mind,' Helgi admitted.

'Fine. But in that case why hasn't he bumped me off long ago?'

2012

Helgi

Sverrir and Helgi were seated in a small meeting room at the police station on Hverfisgata. It was just the two of them. Magnús had made the formal introductions before leaving, but since they had already encountered one another at the door of Sverrir and Tinna's house, the atmosphere was a little strained at first.

'I don't remember seeing you in the police,' Sverrir said after a short silence, his tone polite.

'No, I've been studying abroad and I wasn't with the police very long before that.'

'Ah, I see.'

'Please accept my sincerest condolences. I do hope we can find the person who did it.'

'I hope so too,' Sverrir replied with bitter emphasis. 'I just can't understand it.' After a moment, he went on: 'I'm sorry I was rude to you the other day.'

'Please, don't apologize.'

'Tinna simply didn't want to talk about it. She had nothing to hide. I had nothing to hide. It was just an unpleasant episode we didn't enjoy being forced to rake up.'

'She found both bodies, didn't she?'

Sverrir nodded.

'That must have been pretty traumatic.'

'And that wasn't all,' Sverrir said.

'Oh?'

Sverrir sighed heavily. 'I suppose it can't hurt to tell you about this now. It was completely confidential, just between me and Tinna, but . . . you know, if there's any chance, however tenuous, that her death could be linked to the old case . . .'

Helgi listened without saying anything.

'Basically, what happened is that, after the second death, somebody started stalking her or harassing her, or – I don't know how exactly to describe it – intimidating her, I suppose . . . That's how we ended up getting together, actually, because she turned to me for help. The first incident occurred when she was alone at home – someone tried to peer in her window one night. Then she received a mysterious phone call from the sanatorium late in the evening and we couldn't understand what was going on. Or rather *I* didn't understand – not until long afterwards, when she told me the whole story.'

Sverrir paused for a while, his eyes lowered, his face grey with fatigue, before taking up the story again.

'Of course, I should have told someone about this earlier, but the case had been closed for years and I couldn't betray my wife's trust.'

'I can understand that,' Helgi said, in a sympathetic voice.

'The thing is, she heard someone in the building that morning – the morning Fridjón died . . .'

'In the sanatorium?'

'Yes.'

'There wasn't a word about that in the case files,' Helgi said thoughtfully.

'She kept it secret. I don't exactly know why, except that she was probably – like they all were – relieved that the case had been solved so quickly and easily. Fridjón's death was, well . . .'

'Convenient?' Helgi suggested.

'It's not a very nice way of putting it, but yes, you understand what I mean. The investigation had hit something of a brick wall; we had no leads. Then I arrested Broddi, as you may know. It was a mistake, of course; I acted impulsively. You learn with age. I've often felt bad about the way I locked him up. We didn't have any solid proof against him. Tinna had mentioned seeing blood, but there was no evidence of that . . . I never questioned her about it, but I've sometimes suspected that she might have been exaggerating a bit in her statement.' Sverrir cleared his throat, then went on awkwardly: 'She had a habit of exaggerating or else playing things down; not exactly lying – don't get me wrong – but dressing up the truth. I suppose it stemmed from insecurity.'

'Do you believe she was telling you the truth when she claimed to have heard somebody in the building the day Fridjón died?'

Sverrir hesitated. 'Yes, I'm pretty sure she was. You see, I learnt to read her over the years. I knew when she was inventing things and when she was being straight. And she was genuinely frightened at the time – terrified. Would you like to hear my theory?'

Helgi nodded.

'I've come to believe that Fridjón was murdered. By the same man, or woman, who murdered Yrsa. Tinna turned up unusually early the morning Fridjón died and the murderer hadn't left yet. She didn't see who it was, but the killer might not have known that for sure. They wanted to scare her, to let her know that they were aware of her and that she should keep her mouth shut . . . It worked up to a point too, because she kept silent about it for years. But she didn't know who it was. She just heard a noise.'

The question hung in the air. Could the same person have broken into Tinna's place during the night, while Sverrir was at work, and murdered her? A person who was feeling threatened again, thirty years after the event, because the case had come under scrutiny once more . . . ?

Helgi decided not to ask, though he could see from Sverrir's expression that he was thinking along the same lines.

'How did they get in?'

'You mean the person who . . . who killed her?' Sverrir asked, a catch in his voice.

'Yes.'

'She'd lost her keys a day or two earlier. We didn't think much of it because she was always mislaying them . . . But if someone was watching her thirty years ago, isn't it possible that the same person was watching her again, and stole her keys when the opportunity presented itself? She was forever putting them down somewhere – on the table when she was in a café, for example. She could be a bit careless like that.' Sverrir's eyes narrowed. Perhaps he was wondering whether it had been Helgi's information-gathering for his dissertation that had alarmed the murderer.

If that theory was correct, which of them could it have been? Thorri, the doctor with a secret? Or Elísabet? Or Broddi, perhaps?

Or had Tinna lied? Could she herself have been involved somehow?

Or . . . or could Helgi be sitting face to face with the killer now? Had Sverrir murdered his wife? If so, could he conceivably have played a part in the deaths in Akureyri? The idea seemed impossibly far-fetched . . .

'I should have listened to Hulda,' Sverrir said abruptly.

'Hulda?' Helgi hesitated. 'Is that the woman who was working on the investigation with you?' Come to think of it, he recalled seeing her name in the files.

'Yes. She's bloody sharp. She objected to my arresting Broddi, on the grounds that we didn't have enough evidence. And she tried to convince me to keep the case open a bit longer . . . But I was young and foolish, Helgi. Young and arrogant.'

'Maybe I should talk to her. Is she still in the police?'

'Yes, yes, she's . . . well, I suppose she must be nearing retirement, but she's still working here. Do have a word with her. She can be interesting to talk to, though she's cagey by nature. But then she's been through a hell of a lot – she lost both her husband and her daughter, you know.'

'God.'

'Anyway, definitely hear what she has to say . . .' Sverrir continued. 'I just hope she can be of more help to you than I can.' He looked so tired and defeated sitting there, his shoulders slumped.

'By the way, while I remember . . .' Helgi brought out the old photo from between the pages of his notepad. 'I was wondering if Yrsa could have had a son . . . I don't suppose you remember this picture?' Helgi placed it on the table.

At first, Sverrir didn't seem able to grasp what Helgi was getting at. Then, his frown clearing, he said: 'Oh, I see, you're talking about the photo of the boy you can see at the bottom of the drawer?'

Helgi nodded.

'Actually, I do remember that photo. My memory's not what it was, but I do recall the boy.'

'Was he her son?'

'Oh no. He was Broddi's brother.'

'Broddi's brother?'

'Yes, he got TB and died. He was one of the youngest patients they lost, I believe. Truly harrowing. Naturally, we puzzled over that photo at the time, wondering why Yrsa had held on to it. Whether the boy could have suffered some kind of mistreatment at the hospital, for example, which Broddi felt he had to avenge. Nothing came out of that line of inquiry, but I suppose that's what strengthened my resolve to arrest Broddi. His explanation for what the photo was doing in Yrsa's drawer was that she'd been fond of his brother and his death had saddened her. The staff weren't used to having such young patients at the sanatorium, let alone to losing them. In fact, that was why Broddi went to work there in the first place. He was only a teenager at the time and wanted to be close to his little brother, but of course he couldn't do anything to save him.'

Helgi felt chilled at the thought.

2012

Helgi

It was the same routine as always. Helgi had slept on the sofa, as if he was being punished. They'd barely spoken to each other. Helgi hadn't wanted to talk to Bergthóra and she had left him alone, heading out of the house early in the morning. There were only two alternatives now, he thought: either she could seek help from a doctor or therapist, or he would leave her.

He had pretended to be asleep when she got up, and waited for her to go to work, not moving from the sofa until he'd heard the latch click on the front door.

He was feeling a little nervous about the day ahead. He needed to interview two men, Thorri and Broddi, to find out if they could shed any more light on the case, whether on the recent or on the historical events. First, though, he wanted to have a chat with Hulda, the woman who had worked with Sverrir on the 1983 investigation, in case she remembered something that might come in useful.

He went into the police station shortly before midday, and, having no office to go to, hung around until he could speak to Magnús.

'Hulda Hermannsdóttir, is she on duty today?'

'Hulda?' A flash of irritation crossed Magnús's face. 'She's leaving. Or, rather, she's left. It's her office you're inheriting.'

'What, seriously? Sorry, I hadn't realized.' So it was Hulda who had scribbled down those names on a piece of paper, including the clue that had put Helgi on the trail of Thorri's murky past.

'That's not surprising. I had the name plate taken down from the wall by her office after I hired you. I offered her the chance to retire with immediate effect, but she managed to squeeze a few more days out of me, and . . . to cut a long story short, she's managed to screw that up. It's high time we saw the back of her.'

'Do you think I could have a word with her?'

'I expect so. What about?'

'She worked with Sverrir on the sanatorium investigation.'

'Oh, yes, quite right. Come to think of it, she mentioned something about that. Yes, sure, give her a call.' Picking up his phone, Magnús found and read out her number.

Helgi added it carefully to his phone contacts. 'She's not at work today?'

'No, I've told her not to come back in, so there's no reason why you shouldn't use her office now. Just move her stuff out of the way. I'm sure she'll be round soon to clear it out.'

*

Helgi decided to follow Magnús's advice and take a seat in Hulda's office. He tried ringing her, but her phone seemed to be switched off. No doubt he'd be able to get hold of her later.

Talking to Thorri and Broddi was more of a priority.

When he got through to Thorri, he asked the doctor to drop by the police station for an informal chat over coffee. Thorri had agreed, rather reluctantly, saying he could be there shortly.

It took Helgi several attempts to get hold of Broddi, who invited him to afternoon coffee. So Helgi was faced with the prospect of climbing all those stairs again and doing the whole coffee and Danish pastry thing in the airless flat.

He didn't like to embark on a major clear-out of his new office – not straight away, despite Magnús's claim that Hulda had gone for good. Helgi wanted to give her at least one more day to come by and retrieve her things. On the other hand, he thought, it would be simple enough to make a pile of her stuff and shove it out of the way in a corner. He ran a covetous gaze over the bookcase behind the desk and made plans to bring a few carefully selected titles with him, a tempting collection of Icelandic and foreign detective fiction to dip into when he was in the mood. He knew he would be happy here as long as he had some of his precious books for company.

'I don't need a lawyer, do I?' Thorri asked in a flippant tone, though Helgi could sense the underlying note of seriousness. This didn't necessarily mean that Thorri was worried, only that he wanted to remind Helgi that he had come in voluntarily and deserved to be treated with courtesy. And that, indeed, was Helgi's intention, however delicate the matter he was about to raise with the doctor.

'I don't think there's any call for that,' Helgi replied with composure. 'There's just one thing I wanted to ask you about.'

'Fire away,' Thorri said, lounging nonchalantly in his chair, his legs crossed, as if he had nothing to worry about.

Clearly, the doctor hadn't a clue where this conversation was heading.

'It's about your old job,' Helgi began slowly. 'Before you went to work at the sanatorium.'

'My old job?' Thorri appeared a little shaken. He sat up slightly.

'Yes, in Hvammstangi, you said, if I remember correctly . . .' Helgi left this hanging.

'Hvammstangi, yes . . . Er, did I say that? I meant Húsavík, of course. I was there for a while.'

'Working for Matthías Ólafsson, am I right?'

'Er, yes, for Matthías.'

'Nice guy.'

'You've met him?'

'Young for his age, too. He remembered you well.'

'Yes, naturally I remember him too. He's not the type you forget.' And now there was a slight tremor in Thorri's voice. 'How's he doing?'

'He told me why you had to leave your job.'

'Oh? What did he say?'

'That you'd had a problem with drugs . . .'

Thorri was silent. His expression was a mixture of anger and fear now.

'I . . . I . . . er . . .'

'Just take your time,' Helgi said.

'Look, it was only for a very short period, you have to understand that,' Thorri said at last. He'd uncrossed his legs and was leaning forwards now, his body tense. 'And it never affected my work . . . the patients, I mean.'

'I should hope not.'

'I'd quit before I started at the sanatorium. I was clean by then, and have been ever since. I haven't touched a drug for decades.' This self-confident, arrogant man seemed utterly deflated now. Lowering his head, he said: 'The news mustn't get out. It simply *must not* get out . . .'

'I can understand that. And there's no reason why it should, unless circumstances change . . .'

'I haven't hurt anyone – not a soul, Helgi,' Thorri said, his voice still trembling.

'But I gather,' Helgi continued, 'that Fridjón was aware of your history. And then he died.'

'I had nothing to do with that,' Thorri said vehemently.

'So you're saying he knew nothing about your past?'

Thorri wavered. 'Yes. Matthías told him everything, unfortunately, but – fair play to him – Fridjón was prepared to give me a chance in spite of that. He wasn't necessarily prepared to employ me as a doctor, though. I was taken on initially to research the history of tuberculosis in the north of Iceland. Fridjón objected at first, but eventually agreed that I could join the team.'

'Tell me why I should believe that you didn't want to silence him, Thorri? He knew about your secret and then he went and fell to his death.'

Again, Thorri didn't answer for a moment or two. Then he said, looking suddenly weary: 'Look, we made a deal. He kept his side of the bargain and I kept mine, which means I haven't discussed it with anyone all these years. And I wouldn't have broken my word, but I don't suppose it matters now. It all happened so long ago, and poor Fridjón is long since dead and buried.'

Helgi waited patiently.

'Originally, like I said, the deal was that I'd go to the sanatorium to work on a research project on the history of tuberculosis, and I wasn't expecting it to open any further doors. But then I got wind of a boy, one of the youngest patients to die at the sanatorium . . .'

'Who was this boy?' Helgi asked, though he reckoned he knew the answer.

'Broddi's younger brother. That's why Broddi got a job there while he was still in his teens – to keep an eye on his little brother.'

'But the boy died anyway.'

'Yes, it was a tragic story.'

'Still, wasn't TB more or less incurable at the time? So there wouldn't have been anything abnormal about a child dying, would there?'

'In normal circumstances, no, but there was nothing normal about this case . . .'

'How do you mean? Didn't he die of TB?'

'Oh, yes, he did. Unquestionably.'

'But?'

'I went over all the paperwork . . .' Thorri took his time, pausing to choose his words carefully. 'The archives were perfectly in order, each patient's case history, earlier paperwork, TB diagnosis, treatment, all of it . . .'

Thorri paused for a moment.

'The only problem was this boy.'

'In what way?'

'There was no information to suggest that he'd had TB.'

'What? What are you implying? Didn't you say he'd died of the disease?'

'Yes. But the fact was that he didn't have tuberculosis when he first arrived at the hospital. He was infected while he was there.'

'What are you saying?' Helgi was stunned. 'That's terrible. Was it a mistake?'

'I don't think so. I started looking into the case, without saying anything to Fridjón, because I was touched by the boy's story. Anyway, to cut to the chase, I discovered that Fridjón's brother was the chief constable in Akureyri, and there were rumours that the boy was the chief constable's son. Illegitimate, of course. Apparently, the boy had started telling people that his daddy was a cop, that sort of thing. Fridjón wouldn't admit it, but I always suspected that the boy had been taken away from his mother, who was an unmarried woman from a humble background, and locked up in the sanatorium. To keep him out of sight, I suppose. I'm sure they meant to look after him, but . . . well, we know what happened.'

'What did Fridjón say when you confronted him about it?'

'He admitted there had been a mistake, that the boy had been infected while he was being kept at the sanatorium, but he threatened to expose my drug problem if I mentioned it to anyone. So, I made a deal with him and secured a full-time contract in return . . .' Thorri sat there, head hanging as if in shame.

Helgi was practically speechless. Was this true? Could Fridjón have caused the death of an innocent child?

And, if so, the inevitable question was: *had Broddi known?*

2012

Helgi

Coffee and Danish pastries. No change there, but the atmosphere had shifted, feeling oddly fraught. Perhaps it was the knowledge that Helgi might be facing a murderer, or perhaps he was sensing an increased tension in Broddi, a wariness that hadn't been there before. Could he have his suspicions that Helgi was on to something?

'You're becoming a regular visitor, Helgi,' Broddi said, his voice sounding threadbare, his face drawn with tiredness. He seemed to have aged several years since their last meeting.

'There are just a few points I'd like to go over again,' Helgi replied. 'But I think I've got a pretty clear picture now.'

'Who have you been talking to?'

'Just the usual people, but I had another look at the case files. At old photos of the crime scene.'

Broddi took a sip of coffee, still appearing quite composed.

'What photos?' he asked casually.

'A photo of your brother. The one I mentioned the other day, that was found in Yrsa's desk drawer.'

Broddi nodded.

'I wasn't aware of that. But it doesn't surprise me. He died at the sanatorium.'

'Were you close?'

'Very. He was a sweet kid, always in a good mood, always looking out for me,' Broddi said, his manner still very calm and controlled. 'I don't know if you'd understand, but I was lonely and didn't have many friends, so although I was older than him, I always felt like my brother was taking care of me, just by being there, you know? Just by laughing and smiling and playing with me. We didn't share a dad, but that didn't matter. I remember our games so clearly. We could sit there for hours, amusing ourselves. Then they took him away and put him in the sanatorium.'

'But that's just the way it was, the disease attacked people indiscriminately,' Helgi commented, his face impassive. He wanted to gauge the old man's reaction.

Broddi was silent for a while, staring down at his coffee cup. The Danish pastry was lying untouched in the middle of the table. It looked fresh. Broddi must have gone to all the trouble of climbing down the stairs and going out to the bakery, just to receive a guest who might be coming to arrest him.

'That's right,' Broddi said eventually. He spoke with quiet deliberation.

'You see, it's my belief that the sanatorium staff were cruel to him,' Helgi said after a short silence. He watched the old man carefully. It occurred to him that perhaps he ought to be afraid since Broddi had in all likelihood murdered three people. Yet, strangely, Helgi wasn't frightened. If anything, he felt pity for the man sitting across the table from him.

'They were cruel to him,' Broddi agreed. A coldness had entered his voice.

'And they were to blame for his death, weren't they?'

'I didn't say that.' Broddi's features set in an uncompromising expression.

'They didn't look after him.'

'*No one* could look after him like I could, Helgi. No one.' After a pause, Broddi added: 'They didn't even try.'

Abruptly, he rose to his feet. 'Why are we talking about my brother? I don't want to discuss him. It's all in the past, it's over. I miss him, but can't I be allowed to miss him in peace?' He fixed Helgi's gaze with his own, and again Helgi was seized by a feeling of pity rather than fear. He sensed that Broddi wasn't going to commit any more murders now.

'Sit down, Broddi,' he said sharply. 'We need to have a straight talk.'

Broddi looked taken aback but, after a moment, he resumed his seat at the table and stared unseeingly at his coffee cup, then at the Danish pastry.

'Look, Broddi, I think I know why you killed them.'

Broddi twitched.

'Killed . . . killed who . . . ?'

'Yrsa and Fridjón. I can't say I understand it, of course I don't, but I can put myself in your shoes, at least to some extent.'

'Yrsa and Fridjón? I didn't kill them! Of course I didn't kill them.' Broddi had raised his voice, but his denial was unconvincing.

'And Tinna. You were friends, weren't you?'

'We were work acquaintances.'

'I think you're finding that harder to justify to yourself, Broddi. She hadn't done anything to you. Perhaps she just knew too much. It's easy to make a mistake – a terrible mistake – when you're frightened.'

Broddi didn't speak.

'You are frightened sometimes, aren't you, Broddi? You've known a lot of fear in your life. Fear for your brother. Fear of being found out. I can understand that. It's hard to be alone and—'

At this point Broddi interrupted: 'I told you not to talk about my brother. I asked you not to talk about him.' But his voice had lost its stubborn resolve and now quavered a little, like that of a frightened child.

Helgi was silent for a moment or two, then said: 'But we need to talk about him. Did he have TB already when he was admitted to the sanatorium?'

'He had TB. He'd caught TB,' the old man said.

'Broddi, there's no point fighting any longer. Sooner or later you're going to have to face up to what you've done. Are you really planning to take this secret to the grave with you? Don't you want to try to atone?'

'Atone . . . ?' Broddi lowered his head. It was hard to guess what he was thinking.

'He was a sweet kid, you said?'

Broddi raised his eyes. 'Yes. I've never met anyone better or with a sweeter nature . . .'

'And he understood you, I know that. But it's time to tell this story, Broddi. You can't hide for ever. You've committed appalling crimes and . . .' Helgi broke off, searching for the right words, then continued: 'I believe your brother would have wanted you to come clean now.'

The silence lasted a long time, becoming more charged with every passing second.

'Mum never got over it,' Broddi said finally. 'The TB hit him hard and he went quickly . . . so quickly.'

'Did she know . . . ?'

'She didn't know the whole story, and neither did I, not until Yrsa confessed. But we knew he wasn't ill when they came to take him away.'

Helgi nodded.

'Fridjón's brother was the chief constable, you see. A married man. He was my brother's father. Very concerned about his reputation, the bastard. Didn't want the news to get out that he had an illegitimate son. But my brother had heard the truth somewhere and started telling stories about his daddy being a policeman. A chief constable, even. Of course, people didn't take him seriously because children are always telling stories, but when it came to the ears of the man himself, he decided to take action. He had the boy put out of the way – only temporarily, though. I expect he had plans for what to do with him in the long run, but short term he was kept at the sanatorium, in a closed ward. It was Fridjón who came to take him away from us. Doing the dirty work for his brother. He claimed there was reason to believe he was infected. There was nothing Mum or I could do.'

'Then he goes and gets infected for real while he's locked up . . .'

Broddi lowered his head again. 'It was terrible, absolutely terrible.'

'But you went to work there?'

'At first, it was because I wanted to be near him, see, so I took on some chores – I was only a kid myself at the time – but I wanted to find out what was going on as well. I'd promised my mum that I'd always look after my little brother. I was ten years older than him. And my promise lasted beyond the grave. I had started work there when I was fifteen, doing odd jobs, and later that developed into a caretaker's position. That was fine. The money wasn't bad and I'd never been any good at school. And working there gave me a chance to get to know the people who had killed my brother. All I needed was proof. I had to watch them, try to understand . . . Try to work out what had happened.'

'I see,' Helgi said.

'Yes, I know you understand,' Broddi replied, still a little wearily. 'It was a crime, Helgi. There's no other word for it. A crime to kill an innocent child like that.'

'Do you know what happened?'

Broddi hesitated. 'Yes. Yrsa told me. She confessed in

the end. Told me the whole sordid tale. One of the staff at the sanatorium made a mistake. Her name was Ásta. She didn't know any better – never knew what she'd done, because of course she believed my brother was ill when he was brought in. They'd put him in isolation with orders that he was only to be tended by the two of them—'

'The two of them?' Helgi interrupted.

'Fridjón and Yrsa. No one else knew a thing. Then one sunny day Ásta apparently let him out to play with the other children who were patients there. It was a weekend, so neither Fridjón nor Yrsa was there. And that's all it took . . .' Broddi's voice broke and Helgi noticed a tear run down his cheek.

'When did Yrsa tell you this?'

The ensuing silence was a long one.

'She was about to retire, to leave. I couldn't wait any longer, Helgi.'

'I see.'

'She often went home last in the evening, so I waited for her, more or less ambushed her, and demanded that she tell me the truth. It . . . it took a while. She didn't want to admit anything, but I knew she'd been involved. She and Fridjón always worked so closely together. And she'd always been ill at ease in my presence, all those years – decades – I could sense it. In the end she confessed, but . . . well, not until I'd . . .' He didn't say anything for a moment or two, evidently finding it hard to put it into words: 'I had to use force to get her to speak, as you know. It was worth it, though. To hear the truth at last.'

'Did you mean to kill her, Broddi?'

The old man appeared to think about it. 'I don't really know. Not necessarily, but once she'd admitted it, told me the whole ugly truth, I didn't have much choice but to avenge my brother. And Fridjón had to pay the price for his guilt too.'

'Did you push him off the balcony?'

'Yes, or threw him off, rather. I asked him to meet me up there; fed him some lie about repairs that needed doing. I don't think he'd joined the dots – worked out the connection between Yrsa's murder and my brother's death . . . It had happened so long ago. I expect he was confident no one would ever find out.' After a moment, Broddi added: 'I've never regretted what I did.'

'So, in other words, they arrested the right man at the time.'

'For the wrong reason!' Broddi exclaimed. 'They didn't know anything. They just locked me up because I was an easy target.'

'But Tinna . . .'

Broddi seemed to slump in his chair. 'I'm sorry about that, terribly sorry.'

'What happened?'

'I thought she'd seen me the morning Fridjón died. Because I saw her and she must have heard me. But she never said anything. I tried to intimidate her, to frighten her off going to the police. And it worked. But then you started sticking your nose in and wanted to talk to Tinna. I got scared, Helgi. Scared. I thought she might tell. So I started watching her again and following her. I stole her keys, and entered the house when I saw that Sverrir had gone out. I'm not sure whether I meant to kill her. Perhaps I just meant to talk to her, to make sure she kept quiet. But of course she saw me, and I tried to say something, but she just started screaming and wouldn't stop, and I . . . well . . .'

'You know we need to go to the police station, Broddi. It's all over.'

Broddi looked up and met Helgi's gaze. 'Yes, I know. I'm tired too. I feel terrible about Tinna. I haven't slept much since it happened. I went too far, Helgi. I got carried away. You're right, I need to atone somehow.'

Helgi got to his feet.

'I regret Tinna,' Broddi went on. 'Fridjón and Yrsa deserved to die. Ásta too, but she was already dead by the time I found out. I watched my little brother wither away and die, and it was all their fault. They killed him. You know, people used to call TB the white death because the patients turned so pale. That's how I remember my brother. He was always so bright and cheerful, so alive, but all I remember now is him staring at me through the glass partition at the sanatorium, pale as a ghost, just before he died.'

2012

Helgi

Helgi didn't feel at ease in his new office. He didn't belong there, not yet. It felt as if he were trespassing in somebody else's space, which was true, in a way.

It was late in the evening. Broddi was behind bars and they were awaiting a custody order.

'I expected you to be good, but not that good,' Magnús had told him, and the praise had given him a much-needed boost. Helgi had the feeling he'd found his niche in life.

He'd tried again, without success, to get hold of Hulda. He didn't need her help any more, but he'd have enjoyed telling her that the sanatorium killer had been caught at last, and he also wanted to chase her about clearing out her office. Never mind; she was bound to come in sooner or later.

Helgi had made room for himself at her desk, moving her stuff to one side and putting the largest piles of paperwork on the floor, but apart from that he didn't want to touch anything yet. He'd rather give Hulda a chance to tidy up in her own way, after her long service with the police.

Was it that difficult to retire? he asked himself. So difficult that the woman couldn't bring herself to clear out her office or face facts – acknowledge the cold, merciless ticking of the clock?

Leaning back in the chair, he surveyed the room. There was one photo on his desk – Hulda's desk – of a young girl, her daughter probably, or a granddaughter perhaps. He wondered if he should put a photo of Bergthóra there when the desk became his. If nothing else, he'd bring in some crime novels to fill the bookshelves. Some Agatha Christies, though not the rarest collector's items, a few titles by S. S. Van Dine, and probably his collection of Icelandic translations of P. D. James's series about Inspector Dalgliesh. It felt appropriate somehow to have them with him at the police station.

As his mind dwelt on his beloved books, he was struck by the irony of what had just happened. He had set out to re-examine a cold case from a purely academic perspective, armed with the latest criminological theories, only to end up cracking it by the time-honoured method of interviewing people and following up clues like an old-school detective in one of his whodunnits. All he lacked was the trench coat and hat. He couldn't help smiling at the thought and wondered if he should share the joke with Bergthóra. But no, he doubted she'd see the funny side of it.

This set him off thinking about the evening ahead. He

and Bergthóra were back to square one, fighting and making up. Yet again he was ready to forgive her and overlook what had happened. If she hadn't already gone to bed when he got home, they could talk about the future. They had a variety of decisions to make, such as whether to buy a flat, while their more pressing problems went unmentioned. He knew his patience was close to running out. There were limits to how much more he was willing to put up with.

A sudden deafening blare from the phone on his desk shocked him back to the present. His first reaction, before answering, was to search for a button to turn down the racket. Then he picked up the receiver on the third ring.

'Hello, Helgi Reykdal here.'

There was silence at the other end, then a voice said in English: 'Excuse me, but I'm trying to call Hulda Hermannsdóttir.' It was the voice of an elderly man with a strong American accent.

Helgi answered in the same language, trying to sound polite: 'This is her office, but my name's Helgi.' He wanted to say bluntly that she no longer worked there, but the man on the line sounded like a nice guy and he found himself adding in a friendly tone: 'Hulda is retiring from the police and isn't here at the moment. We're expecting her in the next few days, though. She still has to pack up her things and say goodbye.'

'Ah, OK.' There was a brief silence, then the man said: 'Could you, er, could you take a message for her?'

'Of course,' Helgi replied, reaching for a piece of paper.

'Tell her that Robert called from the US. No, you know what? Tell her that her dad, Robert, called. I'd like to hear from her. She knows where she can reach me. We met one time before.'

For a moment Helgi could have sworn there was a break in the old man's voice, a note of sadness carrying all the way across the Atlantic.

2012

Helgi

It took Helgi ages to locate his house keys, which weren't in his jacket pockets but turned out to be at the bottom of the bag he used for his laptop and the notes for his dissertation. He'd hardly thought about his dissertation all evening, but of course it had developed in a totally unforeseen direction. Solving one murder, let alone three, during the writing of it ought to result in a higher mark, he thought.

He didn't like to knock in case Bergthóra had gone to bed, but he hoped she was still up. They could have a cosy evening together and he could tell her about his day. And what a day it had been . . . He was looking forward to boasting a bit and telling her about the praise he'd earned from Magnús.

When he opened the door and entered the hall, he saw her. She was standing in the middle of the sitting room, her eyes full of hate, just as Broddi's had been earlier. She was holding an empty wine bottle.

'Where have you been?' she screeched. Then, without warning, she was coming at him, brandishing the bottle. Hampered by his bag and keys, he was too slow to raise an arm to protect himself and felt an explosion of pain as the bottle smashed down on his skull.

The world went black.

Acknowledgements

Many thanks to prosecutor Hulda María Stefánsdóttir, my father Jónas Ragnarsson and Lýdur Thór Thorgeirsson for reading and commenting on the text. Thanks also to Eyjólfur Kristjánsson and Sandra Lárusdóttir for the dinner in January 2018 that provided me with the inspiration for several good ideas. I am grateful too to Kaffihús Vesturbæjar, where a large part of this book was written.

And Then There Was Christie

I first came across Agatha Christie's work at around the age of ten. There was a Christie film on television, *The Seven Dials Mystery*, and almost immediately I felt that this was something special, with such a clever twist at the end. A year or two later, my cousin told me that he had started reading Christie's books and praised them highly, so I thought I might give them a chance. I remember the first one I read was *Evil Under the Sun*, in Icelandic translation. A wonderful read, so I kept going. I went to my local library, and lots of other libraries nearby, and borrowed all the translated Christie books I could find, and read them as quickly as I could get my hands on them. (I even started writing my own 'detective stories' at that age, handwritten in a notebook, set in the London fog, very Christie-esque, not realizing that many years later I would actually be writing my own mystery novels.)

And then, suddenly, I ran out of books to read. Not all of Christie's books had been translated into Icelandic, and not all of the translations were widely available. The next stop on my journey was the National Library of Iceland, one of the most majestic buildings in Reykjavík, opened to the public in 1909, located in the centre of town, and a truly lovely place to sit and read. The problem for me was that the great Reading Hall was not open to anyone under the age of sixteen at the time, so I had to almost sneak in with my father, who was doing research there. We spent every Saturday morning in the library, a day when it was open and I was not at school. The memories from then are really wonderful: reading old, out-of-print translations of Christie novels in such amazing surroundings, including what is now my favourite, *The Murder on the Links*.

And then, I ran out of books at the National Library as well! So I ventured into unknown territory, and started reading Christie's books in their original English, enjoying more of her masterpieces.

In Iceland, we have a lovely tradition of giving each other books for Christmas, and then reading our favourite new book on Christmas Eve, by candlelight, into the night. As a result of this, most books in Iceland are published in the months leading up to the holidays, and when I was growing up, an Icelandic publishing house made sure that each Christmas readers had a new Christie translation to enjoy. One summer, when I was seventeen years old, I had a crazy idea – that I could possibly translate an Agatha Christie novel, as I had translated a few of her short stories for a local magazine. My mother drove me to the publishing house, as I didn't have a licence to drive, and I met with the publisher. Surprisingly, he knew who I was, because he realized that I was the boy who had been calling the publishing house every year to enquire which Christie book they were going to publish in translation that year. He greeted me warmly and said that he would give my suggestion some thought. I honestly didn't expect to hear back from him, but he called me back and said that he would give me a chance. I could pick any title, but would need to have a translation ready by Christmas. I rushed to my bookshelves and picked the shortest novel I could find, *Endless Night*, and that turned out to be my first Christie translation.

Translating Christie was a wonderful experience. I carried on translating one a year through college, law school and even after I had graduated and started working as a lawyer. Translating gave me insight into her methods and her magic, and also presented me with memorable puzzles of its own. One clue was so difficult (and in the end, really impossible) to translate that I postponed translating that book for ten years. I won't give away which title, but the clue has a lot to do with the English language, as it relates to a word which has a completely different meaning if one letter is added to it. I looked at other Nordic translations, searching for clues on how translators had gone about making this work in a Nordic language, but to no avail. In the end, I still translated the book, and had to stick to the English words to explain Christie's trick.

There were other interesting challenges in translating her novels in a pre-Google era. For example, I kept wondering why her characters kept walking out of windows, until I realized the true meaning of 'French windows'.

All joking aside, the translations provided me with invaluable experience for my writing career. By the time I had written my first crime novel, I had translated fourteen of Christie's books. To this day, my novels tend to be around the same length as an average Christie book, and that is no coincidence. I also tried to learn as much as I could from her. She created the most beautiful plots, always with a twist at the end. Her detectives were ever so memorable, and her use of setting was unparalleled: the River Nile, the Orient Express, an English manor in the snow – the scene was set for a first-rate mystery, and the setting usually played an important part in the story.

Some people say that Christie took all the best plots away from other authors, and to an extent there is probably some truth in that, although the rest of us keep trying to surprise our readers. A friend of mine, John Curran, who has written extensively about Christie, maintains that the secret of her plots was how simply they could be explained, perhaps in one word or sentence only, yet the readers were almost always taken by complete surprise. I keep rereading her stories, it is impossible not to, if not for the plots (some of which are hard to forget, of course), then simply for the atmosphere she conjures up, transporting the reader to a different place, reminding me of the young boy who sat in the National Library on Saturday mornings, enjoying a great book.

Ragnar Jónasson